Go Forth!

The Band Plays On

BOOK THREE OF THE WEST HOPE TRILOGY

MARY JEAN BONAR

Other books by this author:

Overflowing with Hope, 2008, Tate Publishing Company
Look to the Hills, 2012, Book One of the West Hope Trilogy, WestHope Publishing
Blessed Abbundantly, 2013, Book Two of the West Hope Trilogy, WestHope Publishing

Printed in the United States of America.

ISBN: 978-1-7347977-4-9 (paperback)
ISBN: 978-1-7347977-5-6 (eBook)

WestHope Publishing, LLC
WELLSBURG, WV

"For I know the plans I have for you."
declares the LORD.
"plans to prosper you and not to harm you,
plans to give you hope and a future."

(Jeremiah 29:11) NIV

Contents

Dedication

I dedicate this book to all the women in my life who have taught me life's lessons and have loved me and strengthened me:

To my mother, who has gone through Heaven's doors, and yet remains in my heart and has engendered a great deal of my daily thoughts and actions.

To my Grandmother who lived with us always and was my strong disciplinarian through Christian doctrine and love.

To my daughters, three, who have helped me mature as required, and gave me vision to see through my discipline of them to the beautiful individual personalities each has grown to develop apart from my own.

To my granddaughters who are beautiful inside and out, and are reaching for their piece of happiness in all the right directions.

To my great-granddaughter, who has shown us clearly that the family acquires more beauty down through the generations.

To my Aunts (and there were many) who cuddled me, loved me, and helped me to grow up comfortably, to use proper manners, learn to cook, sew, and care for children, and all the wonderful things that can and should be taught by familiar and loving women of high standards.

I had no sisters or brothers, but belonging to a Church of the Christian Faith, gave me an extended family of sisters who of the same age grew in the faith with me. Others who were older watched over me, all of whom have closely shared the love of the Lord together.

I was invited to join a sisterhood of love, P.E.O., in 1971, and have enjoyed hundreds of sisters locally and across the nation who have grown stronger sharing faith and knowledge with one another.

The older women in my life came to be models of how to face life's sorrows and troubles, and still remain faithful and strong. As I have grown older, I have come to admire and appreciate my opportunities to learn from them. My inspiration comes from them as I have written the books that I have been called to write. One of these beloved gave me a card once that states exactly the words I wish to say to all those mentioned above:

> *"'In my Father's House are many mansions'*
> *♥ I hope yours is next to mine."*

Acknowledgements

I have had opportunities to thank many with the printing of my books, and I could add scores of others because I realize that every personal contact has been a contributing factor in helping me to mature with confidence. Since obviously that feat is impossible, let me say here that I appreciate my family, friends, educators and co-workers for strengthening, supporting, and sustaining my steps forward in many endeavors.

As to writing novels, there are some who have helped in tangible ways. First and foremost, the Lord through the Holy Spirit has prompted me to write this story and guided me through so I definitely give my Lord the praise and the glory for what I found to be a joyful and inspiring assignment. I pray that He is satisfied and that I have completed the work as He has specified for me to do.

There are others in particular: theologians Dr. David Bleivik, and Rev. William Roemer; daughters and protectors Carol Couch and Marianne Cunningham; wordsmiths George Wallace and Mary Kay Wallace—all of whom read through my first manuscript and gave me every encouragement to have it published. I was overjoyed by these responses because I sincerely did not know if my writer's style would be presentable. More than just reading a manuscript, these dear ones read from a box of letter-sized papers one after another. I marvel at their tenacity and kindness yet today, and I love and appreciate them for taking so much time to shuffle through all of those papers to convey to me how they felt about what they read. I knew I had written what I was called to do, but was it rational, well-structured, and enjoyable reading? How thankful I was to hear the words from them that I should have the book printed and marketed.

I also wish to thank Carol Churchman, a dear friend, for reading through the first printing of Overflowing with Hope that I was asked by the publisher to do. She is an excellent fifth-grade school teacher, well demonstrated, as she freely marked those places that needed corrected.

All of this led me to publish and have reason to believe that I should continue the story; however, as health issues arose, I have been delayed until this marvelous day as I am finally realizing the completion of the story and most likely the end of writing such major works—unless and only if nudged by the Holy Spirit to do so.

A small note of additional appreciation: I am now in excellent health and feeling great since I had back surgery. I can sit at the computer and piano, bend and lift and walk; all of which are immense blessings to me.

1

Joy

Janine absolutely could not sleep. She didn't care. It was wonderful to think through the events of the evening and all the days leading up to it. The Kitchen Band had passed the test. The ladies took over the stage, performed like they had been doing that all their lives, and came away all the better for it.

She slipped out of bed as gently as possible, put her feet into her slippers, turned to see if John had been disturbed, and putting her robe over her shoulders, she tiptoed out of the bedroom. She didn't need to turn on any lights as there were tiny night-lights always lighting the way in their home to prevent stumbling. She wrapped the robe tightly around herself and followed the night-lights to her favorite spot on the living room sofa and settled against the cushions there.

Now, she could go on thinking back to the little performance her dear lady friends gave during the evening. Whoever would have guessed that ladies in their eighties—or thereabouts— would step out on a stage, play make-believe instruments, and be so entertaining?

Well, it happened! It did! Janine recalled how she felt last night when she started the music and her beloved ladies marched out to join her. She was thrilled to see jolly excitement in each one of them. They were exhibiting no fear but rather were having a great time of it.

Janine, who was now the leader of the band, never expected to be in this position. If she had thought about it for any time at all, she would have quickly pushed the idea aside. But she didn't think about it. She didn't have to. The Lord Himself plunged her into the classroom that day, and as she talked with the ladies about coming together one day a week to have fun, she had absolutely no idea where that little seed of thought was going.

It was a planting. The seed was small and hardly noticed. Week after week, it grew and developed into an extraordinary entity. It produced delicious fruits of discovery, joy, and delight. The participants, who had been friends for years, now had joined in a new adventure together, and whether it grew any larger or if it became a once-in-a-lifetime moment it was certainly uplifting and would be a notable chapter in a chronicle of memories.

She wasn't tired at all as she sat in the still of the night, not wanting to interrupt her thoughts. Finally, she stood and floated into the kitchen and smiled as she was making a pot of coffee. Waiting for the brew to be complete, she opened the sliding doors to the deck and stepped outside. It was her favorite time of any twenty-four hours.

She was very careful not to make a sound. How quiet it was! She had noticed in the past that the very last part of the night became extraordinarily still, as if the earth was holding its breath before the bursting-forth of the day. She was, in truth, holding hers as well. She turned to go into the kitchen and retrieve her cup of coffee when the very first faint sound came from a bird in the wooded area behind the house. She stopped and, breathing shallow breaths, stayed with the scene.

She closed her eyes in prayer, thanking God for a long list of blessings. She didn't realize that she had been leaning over the rail for quite a while until she finally finished her prayer of thanksgiving and opened her eyes. She didn't really hear the birds until then. They were in full chorus, welcoming the new day, which was colored in soft pastels. She opened her eyes as wide as possible, blinking from the prayer to the actuality of the moment. How many times had she heard the birds singing in the morning? How many times had she seen the breaking of the day? How many times had she marveled at God's creation? She hoped that she would never become blasé and totally unmoved by moments such as these.

The sun arrived and the volume of the chorus increased. The sky turned so bright that Janine couldn't look upon it. As the birds began chirping their way to their daily tasks of gathering, she pulled the robe tightly around her body and went back into the house.

What a beautiful day! What a beautiful life! Janine smiled deeply, thinking again of the ladies, and she hoped that their start to this new day was as joyful as hers.

2

Overflowing with Hope

Janine poured herself a cup of coffee and was surprised to see John come into the kitchen so early in the morning.

"Good morning. I hope I didn't waken you," Janine said.

"No, you didn't. I think I had enough sleep. Did you sleep at all?"

"Not much. I was too wound up, I guess."

"Well, I believe it. You sure had an exciting evening, didn't you?"

"John, I just can't get over it. Wasn't that something?"

"It really was. I cannot believe the talents and creativity of your ladies. And they seemed to have a great time of it too. I can tell you for sure that every one in the audience enjoyed the evening tremendously. The truth is, I didn't expect the band to be that good. No offense."

Janine smiled. Who would have expected it? She poured John a cup of coffee, and they sat down together and talked.

She picked up the cups and carried them to the sink and asked, "What do you have planned to do today?"

"Mr. Lorie called yesterday and said that we finally have a very good prospect to sell our house in town. I knew you had a lot on your mind, so I figured it could wait for me to say something today. It's a young couple. Mr. Lorie said they are very nice and are hoping that we would reduce the price some."

"How much?"

They discussed it and realized that they needed to be finished with the residency in Innesport and it was still a fair offer. They agreed to accept it.

It was a relief after all this time. They had been going back and forth to town to be sure that the house was still in good condition. It had been said that a house deteriorates when no one is living in it, and they really wanted to sell it and know that new lives would occupy the home they had enjoyed for such a long time.

"Okay, I'll give Mr. Lorie a call this morning," John said.

ᘜᘜᘜ

Pauline never did get to sleep last night. She felt so invigorated that she just had to do something, so she found the brass polish under the kitchen sink and shined her trombone until it reflected her smile. She marched around the apartment with it several times, pretending that she was still with the band and the audience was very impressed. She stood the trombone in a safe corner of the living room and finally sat down on the sofa, reflecting upon the evening. She always did enjoy being in the Thespians throughout her high school and college years. Everyone said she was a born actor. Of course, they were right. But who could have dreamed that even now, at the age of seventy-nine, she would be called upon to be a part of a band and entertain again?

Well, never give up. That's what they say. I'm certainly not going to. I have something to do now that will be a lot of fun. In my spare time—when I'm not playing my trombone, of course—I'm going to also concentrate on my oil paintings. I may even paint a picture of a parade with our band leading it. Ha! Why not?

ᴪᴪᴪ

Adele truly felt the blessing. She considered it all an answer to a prayer. She recalled the evening she stood in her window and saw the clouds move over the sunshine, and how the beautiful sunset and rays of sun that evening brought her unexpected hope for something in her future. She had clung to that hope and believed that the Lord was giving her a sign of better days ahead. Could this be that beginning? She smiled and peacefully appreciated the moment as she gave thanks to God above.

ᴪᴪᴪ

"Oh my goodness! It's after eight o'clock. But I had the best dream. I wish I hadn't woken up just yet. Can I get the dream back?" Bea closed her eyes and saw herself back on the stage, blowing her kazoo, dancing around, and laughing like a schoolgirl. She just stayed perfectly still so as to recapture the dream and return for a few more moments of enjoyment.

All of a sudden, she realized that she was *not* dreaming. She actually *did* perform last night. She actually *did* have a great time of it. She opened her eyes, jumped up, and sprinted across the room. She stopped long enough to take a look at herself in the mirror. Yes, she was still that old lady. Too bad, because she felt so much younger right now. She felt like dancing again and laughing and smiling through and through. "Hey! I don't care how old I look. Down deep inside of me is a young girl enjoying life, and I'm not giving up. We're going to have a lot to talk about at Sunday school tomorrow, that's for sure!"

ϒϒϒ

Last night, Owen waited up for Anne to come home from her venture because he wanted to hear all about it. When she came through the door, he knew without a doubt that she had had a good time. She seemed to be filled with spirit and energy such as he had not seen lately.

"Well, how was it?"

"Oh, I guess it was fine." She walked over to the far corner of the living room and deposited her equipment and purse there for the time being.

"Fine? Come on now, you surely can't just say *fine*."

"Well, no one fell off the stage."

"Thank goodness!"

"Yes."

"Is that it?"

Anne sat down, removed her shoes, and ran her fingers through her beautiful white wavy hair.

"Well, we did pretty well, I think." She didn't usually go on and on about anything.

"How so?"

"Well, Bea definitely had fun. She moved around and was laughing and such. And Pauline practically took the stage. You know how she loves to be in the spotlight. But she was really good. Everyone was impressed with that trombone.

"I think Janine was kind of nervous about whether or not we should have tried such a thing. We all were, actually, but Janine seemed to be more so. But in the end, she was really happy. Her family was there too. They thought we were terrific. I wouldn't go *that* far."

Owen smiled. "But did you enjoy yourself?"

"Yes."

Owen was very pleased with that. Anne was a very quiet and subdued person and was not cut out for being in a band by any stretch of the imagination. He had actually worried that she would not enjoy any part of the evening, but apparently she did. How about that?

"You must be tired," Owen said.

"I suppose I am. Would you like some ice cream before going to bed?"

"I just had some, thanks. How about you? Did you work up an appetite?"

"Oh no, I'm fine. We had a very nice dinner. I'll just go get ready for bed."

"All right, I'll be coming too."

After the lights were out, Anne reflected upon the evening with blissful and pleasant thoughts.

Hmm, that was good—good for us and for others as well. We might actually have something here. We'll see.

ϓϓϓ

Like many women her age, Rachael came home to an empty house. She had left the porch light and the hall light on so when Janine and John drove her to the door, no one stumbled. They had talked a lot on the way home about the evening and how special it actually was. Julia was totally shocked that she had been a part of it and said so. She said she never did feel that she was a real part of the community even after all these years.

That just wasn't so, but she couldn't help feeling like it.

As for Rachael, she was so thankful that she had lived after all!

With all her questionings of God as to why she was still here, she still had no real answer, but right now, it just felt right. She believed she still had more of a life to live. It's not just the band. It's a *feeling* of revitalization and happiness she had not known for some time, and it all added up to being here for a reason—whatever that was. Time would tell, and she looked forward to it.

ᘐᘐᘐ

Yes, Julia was somewhat of an introvert and she knew it. Her thoughts that Saturday morning were more of hoping that she did well enough to still be wanted in the band. She didn't know if she did or not.

She was tired last night but inwardly quite happy. She was a part of a group that was very special, and they seemed to include her without any problems.

I really want to stay with it. I can't remember ever having so much fun, she thought.

She was a fine school teacher in her day, and even today, her students stopped by when they were in town to talk with her. Some of the local students did as well. That was a part of her life where she felt that she had truly accomplished something, but being in a group situation with her peers, she never ever believed she lived up to the standards they might be expecting of her. She never would have been a leader but was quite happy to be a follower, and as long as they accepted her, she would give it her all.

Everyone is so talented. I can't even think up an instrument on my own. Thankfully, Rachael suggested the slotted spoon I used in the band. It worked just fine. I'll look around the kitchen and see if there is anything else I might use. They do like the aprons I made, so that's good.

Tomorrow is Sunday, and we'll all be together again. Maybe some of us will go to the Orchard Restaurant after church as usual. Then Tuesday is band practice again, and I'm pretty busy practicing the piano every day, so life is good and well worth the living, I say.

ϓ ϓ ϓ

Saturday morning had always been a good day for Iola. She used to teach piano lessons all day on Saturday but didn't do that anymore since her hearing was so bad, but these days, she used her weekends for studying her Bible lessons and catching up on reading as well. And sometimes there was a good football game or baseball game (her favorite) on television.

That morning, she did not think at all about the reading and her Bible lesson. She was digging through boxes and cupboards, looking for another kitchen band instrument. They were talking about doing a country song, and she had a little brown jug somewhere, and Janine thought that would be utterly fantastic.

Of course, she never did drink any kind of hard stuff like what goes into a little brown jug, and she wondered if everyone would think she was someone who might imbibe in the shadows or something, so she was uncertain if she really would like to contribute the jug. Maybe not, but it sure would produce a good laugh, and maybe it would be okay to hand it off to someone to blow into.

She had a really good time at the installation of the new pastor last night. She enjoyed everything about the evening: the service, the dinner, the fellowship, and much to her surprise, the band.

This could be the start of something. Probably not, but it could, I suppose. I think I'd like that.

She couldn't believe her own thoughts. This was definitely not the way she expected to spend her time in these senior years. After all, she had always been upright and strongly sure of what was right and wrong about being a Christian. Now here she was, dancing and playing stupid instruments in front of people. *What kind of influence is that going to be, and should we be doing such a thing?* The ministers who were at the dinner last night all loved the program. They felt that the band was a good means of spreading the love of the Lord and sharing in fellowship and laughter together.

O Lord, I hope we were not an embarrassment to You. Guide us into always doing the right thing, and if we are not, just smack us down.

She continued to look for the jug, feeling pretty good about it all, and beginning to believe that Janine was right about the Lord calling them into an effective way of service.

3

Overflowing with Promise

She looked at the result bar on the testing device. She had waited the required three minutes by counting slowly to 180 while keeping her eyes closed. She paused, drew in a deep breath, held it, and then peeked out into the room. The hand holding the tool was trembling as she slowly looked down at the results.

"Is that a plus or a minus?"

She couldn't really see it. She blinked several times and lifted the device closer to her eyes.

"It looks like a plus. It is! I'm pregnant!"

She marveled that she was truly excited and happy. She had not planned on having children thus far. *"I wonder why? I love children. I have worked with children and seen my sister's children grow and enjoyed every event and occasion possible with them. Why had I not felt that it was time for us to be parents? I have wonderful parents. I think I would be a good parent."*

Yes, indeed, she would be a great parent, and her children will love her, and life will be complete as they grow up in such a loving home. *They?* Of course! We'll have a houseful!

Now, now, girl. Settle down. You are flying so high right now that your thoughts are exploding. One child at a time.

She turned to the mirror. *Do I look any different?* she thought. *I should. I feel extremely different at this moment. I can't remember ever feeling so full of joy and warmth and all the cuddly things encircling and embracing me right now.*

She was beaming. Her cheeks were flushed, and her eyes were sparkling. She actually did look different. She turned sideways, arched her back, and rubbed her hands over her flat tummy.

"Little baby, little baby, you are right here inside of me. I love you already. I love you with everything in me because you are a part of me and your daddy." *Your daddy! I wonder if he could possibly understand this joy. Do men really have the ability to feel this ecstasy?*

She held her tummy and closed her eyes and rocked side to side, soaking in the loveliness of her sensation.

"Hello! Hello! Hey, where are you?"

She was awakened from her dreamworld, and even though she wanted to continue rocking and humming, she turned on the water and responded to him that she would be right out.

"Hi," he said as he kissed her cheek. "I'm finished at work for the day. Are we still going to Kathy's?"

"Of course. It is a beautiful day for a picnic, and it will be a perfect time to make an announcement."

"What announcement?"

"You are going to be a daddy."

"What? Are you serious? Wait! Are you sure?"

"Yes, I'm sure. I just tested, and the results were clear that we are going to have a baby. Oh, Robert, I hope you can be as happy about this as I am. What are you thinking?"

"I'm thinking this is great news—the best news. Wow! I wondered if this would ever actually happen."

"It has," she said as he reached out for her and embraced her lovingly.

"We'll tell the family today. I couldn't possibly wait to make a big production of the announcement. We'll just burst in and let everyone in the family know," Deborah said.

"Yes. Yes, I agree. This is too good to keep to ourselves. You should make an appointment with Dr. Doloria as soon as you can."

Deborah smiled. "She's really going to be surprised. I saw her a couple of months ago for my annual checkup, and she asked me when we were going to get started with our family. I told her I didn't know but not right away. You know, I really hadn't thought that much about it, but now at this moment, I can't imagine why."

4

A Basketful

Janine had to hurry. She had been so absorbed with her thoughts of the band's performance last night that she had gotten a bit behind in peeling the apples for the pies. John agreed to peel them for her before he went into town to talk with Mr. Lorie. One wondered if he would have been so eager to do so if they hadn't found that fantastic apple peeler last year. He actually enjoyed putting the apple on the post and turning the handle around and around while the peelings curled off and the slicer sliced at the same time.

"I wish I knew the person who invented this. It's actually fun to use," John said.

"It had to be a man."

"Of course, it was a man—a man with a very sharp mind and little time to fiddle around the kitchen."

"I always liked to peel my own and see if I could peel one entire piece of the skin from beginning to end without it falling in two," Janine said.

"Well, challenges do make the work more enjoyable."

"Yes, and sometimes opens one up to invention, I suppose. But nevertheless, I appreciate your help here. I almost forgot that we were going to Kathy's today. Last night, she said 'See you tomorrow,' and a light went off. Thankfully, I already had gotten the apples from the orchard. Marcia asked me if I would be baking pies and wanted to know which apples I had decided worked best."

"Did you tell her?"

"Of course. She agreed too."

"Well, even if she uses the exact recipe, still no one can bake a better pie than you do, Janine."

"Thanks, hon. Of course, the more you say that, the more pies you will be getting. You're a really smart guy, you know."

"Yep, but I'm telling you the truth."

He finished with the peeling while Janine worked up the dough, and in no time, the pies were in the oven. John went off to see Mr. Lorie, and Janine went about cleaning up and gathering what she needed to take to the picnic.

Kathy, Greg, and the two girls—Karen and Meghan—were all set up in back of the house when Prince perked up, jumped like a rabbit, and headed quickly around the house. The little family knew for certain that company was comin'.

It's Grandma and Granddad! Yay! Prince thought as he realized who was there.

He went straight for them and knew they were going to give him lots of good hugs and a rub or two. He responded by licking them and squeezing up tight against their legs.

Everyone loved Prince. And why not? There wasn't a better dog on earth, of course. He was a black lab, fully mature, with fine manners and was very, very handsome too.

They family wasn't far behind, and they gathered up the items that were in the car and headed around the house.

"What a beautiful day for a picnic," John said.

"My goodness, yes. And look at the setting. Who made all these decorations?" Janine asked.

Karen and Meghan were bursting with pride as they quickly said that they had done all of them.

There were huge paper flowers in a variety of colors hanging from the trees, and the color scheme was carried through to the tablecloths and paper flowers on the tables as well, very festive. It was no special occasion except that they would all be together, which always seemed like a celebration in the family.

Kathy asked Janine how she felt after that great presentation last night, and Janine broke into her beautiful smile and enjoyed talking about it all over again. It was just so great that Kathy had been there to share in it with her.

Greg was beginning to put something on the grill. Who knew what it might be, but whatever he cooked was always unbelievably delicious, so everyone just left him to it and waited for the surprise. Soon the aromas began to waft through the yard, and questions just had to be answered. Yes, he was cooking his famous marinated chicken breasts. Everyone cooks marinated chicken, but he does something so special to his that sends everyone diving for a piece as soon as possible.

Prince jumped! Deborah and Robert were coming.

I'm coming. I'm coming! Prince was saying as he barked and barked, running around the house and practically jumping into their waiting arms.

"Oh, Prince, Prince, Prince. I love you. Let me hug you," Deborah said.

Hey, something special is here. What is it? It makes me feel warm and important, Prince was thinking.

He stayed as close to Deborah as he could all around the house. He kept looking up at her and wanting to know what she knew, but didn't know how to get any answers.

Deborah really didn't profess to be a great cook, but she sure knew where to find the most delicious foods in the delis of any fine store in the entire area. She brought cheeses and crackers and a watermelon!

All was near ready, and after some hugs and kisses, Deborah said, "Hey, everyone, listen up. Something very special is going to happen."

So of course, she immediately had their attention.

No one guessed. Some thought they were going to move into a house closer by as it had been discussed lightly at an earlier time. Others were thinking of France and their connections there, but no one actually thought it was news about a baby, so when she blurted out "Robert and I are going to have a baby," everyone froze in their tracks for a few minutes, catching their breaths.

Prince still was cuddling up as close to Deborah as he possibly could, and she kept touching him in a mothering sort of way.

Who would be the first to speak?

"So, the cycle of life continues," John, the philosopher, said.

Janine began to cry, the girls were jumping up and down, Greg put down his cooking gear, and Kathy ran to Deborah and embraced her for a long, long time. The sisters shed loving tears of understanding with one another.

Everyone was happy. It was a good moment, and everyone knew it was the right moment even though no one had previously applied a mathematical formula to the days or years when it should or would happen. It just did. And the family embraced it all as God's gift to them.

ϒϒϒ

"When is the baby due?" Janine asked.

"We just found out today. I mean, I took a pregnancy test and found out. I have to make an appointment with Dr. Doloria. I think I may already be a couple of months along. Can you tell?"

"Heavens, no. Except you have that glow about you. I might have guessed if I'd had a little more time. I'm pretty good at that," Janine said.

Karen and Meghan began to hold hands together and skipped around in a circle, singing "I'm going to be an auntie.

I'm going to be an auntie." They said they would help with babysitting, and Deborah realized that the girls certainly would be very helpful.

"We should move to a house with a yard like yours," Deborah said, and Robert agreed.

Deborah smells so nice, Prince was thinking. He was still right beside her.

"I think Prince knows something is different," Kathy said.

"Probably," said John.

When John and Janine were in the car going home, Janine said, "How many times in life do we have such a perfect day as today?"

"Not very often, I suppose, but it seems we've had more than usual lately, don't you think?"

"Yes, but life is hard, making these moments more appreciated. When I was a little girl my mother told me that," Janine said.

"Told you what?"

"That life is hard. I was thinking at the time that life should be happy, happy all the time, and I guess there was some sort of incident that made me very sad, and I probably couldn't understand why that should happen to me. So she said, 'Life is hard, Janine.'

"I certainly must have asked why life had to be hard, because I was so young and foolish. She was a wise lady. She told me that I might as well face up to it. Life is hard most of the time—probably ninety-five percent of the time. But she also said that the other five percent of the time life is so overwhelmingly wonderful that it makes up for all the troubles we encounter."

"She was right, I suppose. When you think of all the troubles and difficulties we find as we go along, it's a lot. But, Janine, you and I have truly been blessed, haven't we?"

"I'd say so! For one thing, we live in a country where, so far, our freedoms have not been taken from us. It would be a completely different world if we lived under tyranny. Then *every* day would be difficult. And, John, more importantly, we have our faith, which lifts us up above the trials with the knowledge that the Lord is with us and looking after us."

"As long as we look to the light, Janine, we won't be living in darkness."

"Um-hmm." She loved it when he quoted things, whether or not they might be fundamentally true to a key wording or made up to suit the thoughts he had. *John the Philosopher.* The head of the household. The true rock of the family. She smiled in gratitude for him and for her family as well. *God is good. He takes care of our every need, and we have much more than five percent of the allotted good that my mother spoke of.*

5

Who Knew?

Each and every one of the ladies of the band arose early to go to church. The hands of the clocks were so slowly turning that morning that it seemed they would never leave the houses and get to talking with the others about Friday evening. But soon enough, they were into a conversation that was quite invigorating and joyful.

Harriet, the Sunday school teacher, was so fascinated with the conversation that she let them talk for at least twenty-five minutes before she just had to go to the assignment.

"There was this one man who introduced himself as the pastor of one of the churches—I don't remember which—who said that he never laughed so much. He said that we should go spread the love of the Lord throughout the area."

"I heard words like that too. I'm actually shocked at the reaction of the people."

"Me too. I never dreamed that I could be an entertainer. Some of you are more cut out for that than I am. But I loved it. I can't believe it. I hope we can do it again some time."

"Well, we did pretty well for ourselves. Janine seemed happy too."

"It was a good time. It probably will be something we can think about for a long time."

Harriet was so impressed when they told her how they actually got on the stage and did the songs and moved about in style. Someone asked her if she could free herself up from some of her volunteer works to come and be a part of the band, but she couldn't see any way at the moment. She realized that she was missing out on something really fun instead of constant involvement in serious work.

Well, it is what it is, she thought. *Maybe someday.*

Also Virginia stopped by the classroom. She had overheard a church officer talking to a group about the Kitchen Band when she had come through the doors. They were all listening intently as he told them about Anne, Bea, Iola, Rachael, Adele, Julia, and Pauline having made history last Friday. No one could believe it!

"Surely, not Anne Kendrick! She is so quiet and reserved."

"Talk about reserved. Julia Gillanders? Julia was on that stage? Good grief! I can't believe it. What on earth got into them?"

The officer replied, "I think the question should be, 'Who got into them?' It seems the Holy Spirit was moving about.'"

"What? Are you serious?"

"Well, it sure seems to be the answer. How else could we explain something like this, and Janine told the group assembled that the Lord had called them together to be a band!"

"Wow!"

"I know."

"I can actually visualize Bea Roberts enjoying being a part of an entertainment group. She probably had the time of her life. She always was one to throw herself into any kind of fun situation."

"Yes, that's true. But I was there. They were *all* like that. They all were enjoying themselves thoroughly. It was great fun to see. And the audience really got into the swing of it all."

Virginia couldn't believe her ears, so she peeked into the classroom with her sister in tow and saw that the gals were in such busy conversation that she should probably not interrupt. She left to go sit into the sanctuary with Elrita. Sometimes it took Elrita a bit of time to adjust to her surroundings, and she probably would be more than confused to hear the excitement in that classroom.

The ladies tried to pay attention to Harriet as she summarized the lesson for the day, but it was hard. They were energized and needed to move around some. As soon as the prayer ended with the *amen*, they all jumped up and scurried out of the room, into the hall, and chatted some more, mainly because they couldn't get away from friends stopping them to ask questions about the performance.

The organ began to play the prelude, so they all knew it was time to turn their attention to the service and focus upon the real meaning of the morning. Each member of the band was smiling all the way to her seat as the music played a joyful Mozart classic.

As for Janine, she felt the Lord's presence, and her music expressed her thankfulness.

6

Everybody's Talking

Marcia scurried to the restaurant after church to help serve as they were a little short of help. She put her apron on and lent a hand in the kitchen. All of a sudden, there was a great commotion in the dining area. *What's going on?*

She looked out and didn't notice any problems, so she went back to the cooking. The waitress, Jackie, told her it was a good thing she was there because they had a larger crowd than usual.

"Have you heard about the band?" she asked Marcia.

"What band?"

"The band from Hope Church?"

"No, there is no band at Hope Church. We have a very traditional and conservative church, Jackie. We wouldn't go for a band in church."

"No, not a church band really. A band consisting of ladies from Hope Church."

"Ladies from the church? I don't know what you are talking about."

"Well, you're going to find out. They have caused quite a stir in the community, and word has it that they are great entertainers and will probably be famous some day."

"My goodness! What on earth . . . ?"

"Well, the ladies are in their special room. Maybe you would like to go talk to them and find out for yourself."

"Okay, I will. I'm caught up here right now. I'll be back in a few minutes."

Marcia was pleased to see the ladies all excited about something. It was quite unusual.

"What's this I hear? What have you gals been doing lately?"

"Oh, it's nothing, really. All we did was go to the installation of a new pastor, and we did a little entertaining. Everyone is so surprised that we old fogies can still do something fun, I guess, so they are all just going on and on about it. It won't amount to anything," Iola said.

"Yes, you know how things can get exaggerated," Anne interjected.

"Well, what did you do?" asked Marcia.

"Well, we've been having an interesting time of getting together on Tuesdays and came up with some music to play with kazoos, that's all," said Rachael. "People are just making a mountain out of a molehill."

"You got together and went to the installation and played kazoos?"

"Yes. It sounds about as crazy as it was, but somehow it became entertainment in some strange sort of way," Julia said.

"Oh. Well, that's very interesting, anyway. I never would have guessed that."

"Who would?" Bea asked. "But I'll tell ya, ya had to be there. We had a blast, and the audience went crazy. It's as though it was meant to be. I can't explain it. I wish we could do it again and again, though. It was so much fun."

Everyone agreed.

Marcia was stupefied and decided not to ask any more questions about the band.

"Did Jackie get your order?"

"Not yet."

"I'll go tell her to come around. Have a great day, ladies."

They ate their favorites, sat a long time together, and finally had to go on their way—most to an empty house once again. However, things were different that day. Everyone left smiling and seriously looking forward to being together again Tuesday morning.

7

Little Brown Jug

Iola had to talk to herself over and over to be convinced that it was okay to take the little brown jug to practice. She wrapped it up in a towel and stuffed it down into the bottom of her bag with the other supplies.

"Maybe I'll take it out and maybe not."

When they settled down after their greetings to one another, Janine gave a little prepared speech to them about her satisfaction with the performance and her recognition that they are definitely called to work in the Lord's service. "Pray and be prepared to follow His lead."

They all secretly hoped very much that they could be a group to do just that and soon!

They went through the routine, discussing a few minor changes in the presentation, and decided that they should not give up on the practices and should be thinking of anything that might increase the entertainment value of what they were doing.

Iola asked, "Are we going to go ahead with a country song?"

Janine said, "I think it would be a good addition. Any ideas?"

At that, Iola pulled out her jug!

It was a shock to everyone. Where would she have gotten that?

She said, "I have no idea where this ever came from, but I can play bass on it, unless one of you would like to give it a whirl."

Silence.

"Okay, I can do it, I think."

Janine, was so tickled, it was all she could do not to jump up and down. Iola, of all people. She, the ultra strict, upright, and proper?

But Janine held all of it in, and suggested calmly that the rest of them think about getting straw hats, and she would work up a song.

That was an assignment, apparently, and everyone would certainly figure out about the hats, and Iola said she would practice! It really would be fun just to see Iola participate in such an act. These "sisters of the faith" had become closely entangled with their delights and their achievement. Everyone had an attitude of hope and expectancy. A candle had been lit, and life was good.

Maybe a bit of that five percent has fallen upon them. The thought suddenly flashed across Janine's mind.

8

It Begins

"We have an invitation to entertain again." Janine was attending another practice with the ladies of the band.

"This is from the Green Valley Homemakers. They want us to come to their Tuesday evening meeting in two weeks. They have offered us a covered-dish dinner provided by the homemakers and want us to come early. Where do they meet?"

"That's on the south side of town in a refinished barn there. It's a very neat place, and homemakers from all around have joined up to meet occasionally to get to be better acquainted. Rachael, don't you go there?" Anne asked.

"I used to when I felt like it. I actually haven't returned to meetings since my accident. It would be a pleasure to see everyone. This is quite a nice surprise. Can we go?"

It didn't take long to agree to participate. After all, the ladies rarely had many appointments on their calendars except for doctor visits, so it was easily and quickly decided.

They had a country song now. Iola must have practiced a lot because she was very good at the bass part. Bea brought a really snazzy-looking ukulele made from shiny pie pans with bright stickers all over it. Her hat was frilly and labeled with a hanging price tag of ten cents, typical of Minnie Pearl's of the Grand Ole Opry. Leave it to Bea!

Everyone did a great job with the hats with bright-colored field flowers and hay, and miniature garden tools dangling, and other interesting gadgets. They just couldn't be topped in their creativity.

Pauline said they still need a good name. Everything from the kitchen was suggested, but nothing was settled upon. Rachael said that ever since they began, the members felt that hope was growing for them. "Could we be called The Band of Hope?" Everyone liked that. It said a lot about who they were and what they wanted to carry into the world as well.

ᲧᲧᲧ

They were a hit at the homemakers meeting, and a few asked if they had a business card. Ha! Cards—that's a good idea.

Janine said she had seen a site online that made business cards and she would get some that said The Band of Hope.

The entertainment schedule was filling up for the summer months. They went to a senior center in a nearby community and a reunion for the high school class of '46! Wow! And yet they were nearly the same age as some of the band members. The band added some songs of that era, and the reunion folks sang along with the ones they knew. It was a great time.

There were more requests. The scariest one of all was to entertain at their own church annual picnic at a local park. Here was the test! It could go very badly. Even Jesus was tested by the hometown crowd. At the very least, it was difficult to convince people who knew you very well into believing that you can be professionally qualified in your endeavors. But they packed up instruments as well as salads, desserts, or whatever they normally take to the picnic, pushed aside their apprehensions, and attempted to reintroduce themselves to well-known friends and families as The Band of Hope.

It didn't go nearly as smoothly as all the other missions. Things broke, not all were in step, the electrical outlet was too far away for the music box, and the sound system was horribly inadequate. But they stood up to the tornado of twists and turns, played those kazoos with everything they had, danced harder, laughed deeper, and in the end won over the crowd overwhelmingly. Even the youngest children loved the entertainment. Nothing could stop them now!

9

Be Here—Go There

Janine was being pulled in two directions these days. She was having a better time than she could remember with the band and also was doing all that she could to help Deborah move into her new home nearer the borough. Unfortunately, Deborah was not having the best of days. She had been very sick every morning for a few months. Sometimes it eased off during the afternoon. Deborah was having a sonogram this week to learn more about the baby. She was extremely happy in spite of the sickness and the sudden weight gain. She decided against going back to teaching in the fall, and was glad of it. She could not get enough sleep and didn't think she was alert enough to be an effective teacher. Robert, of course, was eager to help her whenever he could. He slacked off for some hours in the office to be of help to her and to enjoy every minute of the pregnancy that he could. They both felt the blessing that was given to them and didn't want to rush through it unaware of everything that was happening.

Dr. Doloria informed them that everything was fine, but she was not surprised when she witnessed the sonogram and could see two definite forms in the womb. When she announced to Dr. Franklin and his wife that they would be birthing twins, they were all ecstatic.

The babies were not positioned as Dr. Doloria preferred, and she informed them that they could come a little early. The due date was moved from March to perhaps weeks earlier. That was not a problem for them. They had a nursery the size of family room! It was already furnished, and they would just go out and duplicate what they had already purchased.

"Can you tell if they are boys or girls?" Robert asked.

"I can pretty much tell you, if you want to know," she responded.

"Let's wait for now," said Deborah. "We have really great news today. Let's save some for later."

Dr. Doloria did tell Deborah that she truly believed from what she was seeing that Deborah would more than likely have to go in the hospital or to a bed with full-time care for the final trimester of the pregnancy.

Robert was thinking that he probably would not be able to take off work that amount of time and that Deborah could go into the hospital. He would watch after her regularly.

Deborah didn't care one way or the other. She was overwhelmed with excitement that they were going to have twins. She prayed that God would take care of them and protect them throughout the pregnancy and the birth. She knew she would do everything she could to see that her children were healthy all the way and always.

ϓϓϓ

When Deborah and Robert got to the car, she quickly called her mother.

"Mom, guess what!"

"What?"

"Looks like we are having twins."

"Oh, my Lord. John! John! Come here."

"What's wrong, honey?"

"Nothing, I want to tell you something. Hold on, Deb."

"Guess what?" Janine asked John this time.

"What?" John asked.

"Deb and Robert are going to have twins!"

Deborah wished she could see in the parent's room. "What is he saying?" she asked her mother. Robert was also eager to hear what John would say.

John was standing very still, staring straight ahead for several minutes.

"Wait, Deb, he is garnering his thoughts. In the meantime, I myself am very, very happy and excited. Boys? Girls? One of each? What do you know?"

"We don't know yet. Now what is Dad doing?"

"He has turned to me with something to say. Wait, please."

Finally John said, as only John can, "Life will be two-rific with twins."

"Why don't you come over and let us give you big hugs? I can't wait to talk with you face-to-face," Janine said.

"Robert, can we swing around to Mom's for a while?"

"Sure!"

Deborah was feeling great at the moment. Everything she looked at out the car window was beautiful in her eyes. She imagined driving on the road with her two babies in the car seats and even had to resist looking over her shoulder to get a view of how that would appear later on.

She was so thrilled over the fact that they would have one baby—and now two. What a joy!

"We'll be very busy, Robert."

"Of course! We will, but so have millions of other parents. We'll be fully up to it."

"I know we will. We should have thought of being parents earlier. I think I should resign my job. The board can begin looking for a replacement. It's a fact that I won't have time for anything once these little darlings come into our lives."

"I'm glad you said that. I've always been a pretty strong proponent of mothers staying with their own children whenever possible. We want our children to be taught the ways of the world as we see it—as we believe—and we can afford for you to stay at home. But do you think you can just stop teaching all of a sudden?"

"Robert! I most certainly can! I can't think of anything more important than being with my babies. I'll teach them proper manners and how to read—well, maybe not right away." She laughed as she realized how far she had gotten ahead of the circumstances. The future seemed to be upon them in her mind and heart. She could not remember being so full of happiness, and she knew the true essence of motherhood within her.

In the meantime, Janine called Kathy and invited them to stop over for a little while. She knew her girls. They would want to also be together at a time like this.

"Sure, I'll be there in a jiffy. Greg's working and the girls are spending the day riding horses at the neighboring farm. I'll bring Prince."

Janine had not told her the news. Prince was knocking at the door with Kathy, and they both came in together. Prince always knew he was welcome at Grandma's house.

"Would you like something to drink? Coffee?"

"No, thanks. Did you have something to talk about, Mom?"

"Not really. Deb and Robert are coming, and I thought you'd like to see her today."

"I sure would. She was going to the doctor today, wasn't she? Is everything all right?"

"Of course, everything's all right. Did the two of you find the right paint swatches yesterday for her house?"

"No, not really. That's a pretty big house. I don't know if I would have the energy to take care of it. I hope she knows what she's getting into. She'll be fine with it, and I'm so glad they have moved nearer to us."

At that, the car pulled up, and Prince was immediately at the door waiting.

Here's Deborah! Prince wagged and circled and let her know how happy he was.

"Hi, Mom. Hi, Kathy. I'm glad you are here. And, yes, Prince, I love you too!"

Janine hugged her as much as she dared. "Come sit down. Would you like some cool water or something?"

"No, thanks. Robert, would you like to go get a cup of coffee for yourself? I know the pot's always on here."

"Right. I'll go get a cup. Where's John?"

"He's back there. Bring him back with you," Janine said.

Deborah sat on the sofa with her mother, and Kathy sat in a chair where she could enjoy the conversation.

"What's the news?" Kathy asked.

Deborah and Janine looked at each other smiling. John and Robert walked in, carrying their coffee mugs, and just stood.

They kept smiling and somehow knew that John would be the one to speak up, so they waited.

John said, "Something two-rific has happened."

Kathy wasn't sure she heard him correctly. She frowned as she pondered what he actually said. She looked over at Deborah, who was being cuddled closely by Prince. "Hmm, what did you say?" No one said a word. They knew she'd get it soon enough. When she did, she said, "Wait a minute." She walked over to Deb, looked her straight in the eyes, and said, "Twins."

Deborah nodded enthusiastically.

"I knew it!"

10

Prince Has a Vacation

Deborah felt better when the very hot days of summer changed into a refreshingly cool period. The babies were becoming a bit active then, and she found that a few naps each day helped tremendously. She and Robert shopped online for household necessities instead of going through stores and completed the twins' room. If anyone had been given the opportunity to take a look into the room, they would have known that girls were coming again. Pinks and cream and lace on the borders of the walls, curtains of bouffant, baby dolls sitting in a little rocking chair of pink with flowers all over it and more and more fun things to add as time was going along.

Kathy was coming over to drop Prince off today because she and Greg and their girls would be taking a few days for a trip to the beach. Prince didn't want to go, and he certainly had a place to stay.

"Are you going to let Kathy see the room?" asked Robert.

"I think so. I'm terrible at keeping secrets, and anyway it's fun to share. I'll show Mom and Dad too, right away. We have everything looking so sweet and welcoming."

Standing behind her, he wrapped his arms around her waist and kissed the back of her neck, overcome with emotions of love and tenderness toward her. She turned, looked up into his eyes, and buried her head into his neck. They stood there for quite some time with the realization that they had been blessed abundantly. As they went into their part of the house, their feelings increased, and they shared physically what they felt within. There are times—yes, perfect times—when life is truly worth living and sharing.

ΥΥΥ

What's this? Where are we? I can't smell anything familiar here.

Prince had been riding in the family car with his nose out the window. After leaving his natural environment, nothing seemed familiar, actually. And now, here they were, stopping at some strange place. *Why?*

"Come on, Prince. Let's go find Deborah," said Greg.

Deborah? Oh boy! Deborah. But why is she here? Oh well, I don't care. I want to see her now." He jumped out of the car and started toward the house. He abruptly turned and ran back to his family. *Come on, come on. Let's go.*

They scurried to him, and they were at the house just as Deborah opened the door.

Here she is! Here she is! I am so happy. I think she is so special, and she has a secret that she hasn't shared with me yet. Maybe she will today. Mmm, mmm, she smells great.

Something different is happening, and I want to know more. I want to know more.

"Prince, Prince. There you are. Do you know you are going to stay here with us for a few days?" Deborah asked as she ruffled his fur and hugged him.

I'm going to stay with Deborah? That will be so good. Yes, yes.

"I'm positive he understands anything we tell him," Kathy said. The girls agreed. "We brought his box with his food supplies and a couple of toys, and of course, his Frisbee. Be careful though, or he'll wear you out with that."

"I know how he is. I need some good exercise anyway. We'll have a great time together, won't we, Prince."

We will! We will! He began to calm down and hold his side against her leg.

"He's just the best," Deborah said.

"Well, if you haven't any questions, we are ready and rarin' to get going. We'll have our cell phones. You have all four numbers, so call anytime you want," Kathy said. "Are you feeling well? Are you sure about having Prince here?"

"I feel better all the time, and I can't think of anything else I'd rather do right now than to have my sweetest buddy here with us for a few days—or forever!"

"Now, now. Don't get carried away," said Kathy. "But I feel sure you will enjoy each other."

The Langs hugged their precious dog and were anxious to get going. When they were on their way, Robert asked why she had not taken them to see the nursery, and she said it wasn't a good time. They needed to go for the girls' sake.

Prince watched them go, cocked his head, looked at Deborah, and quietly asked, *What's going on here?*

"Come here, Prince. Let me give you a big hug. You'll be staying here with us for a while. Don't fret. Things will be good. Let's go inside."

Okay! Me first, " he said as he went through the door. *Hey! This is cool. I like this place. Where's the kitchen? Oh, here it is. What's over there? Oh, lots of rooms to explore. Yay.*

Robert and Deborah just watched his shenanigans and almost laughed out loud. He was going to have fun in this place. They had shut the nursery door. He wouldn't be going in there.

It took him a while to calm down and get a feel for the house. He found his friends in the family room settled down on comfy furniture, and so he got as close to Deborah as he could and curled up in his favorite position and went off to sleep. It was a good feeling for the three of them.

Prince jumped up! *What was that?*

Deb jumped too. Her little darlings were having a territorial battle inside, it seemed. She couldn't get them to calm down, and Prince somehow knew what was going on.

He sat on his haunches, ears perked, head tilted, and with a very curious and questioning look on his face. *What did Deborah do? I just don't know. I just don't know.*

"Robert, look at Prince. He knows the babies are moving about. Could they be making sounds that are detected by him?"

"I have no idea, but if he would look at your tummy, he would see where it is coming from. Wow! How do you feel about that?"

"I love it! It doesn't hurt. It's just wonderful, actually. It could get more difficult as they get bigger, I suppose. But for now, it's just fine. It's really early for them to be so active. We may have our hands full with these movements later on."

11

New Paths, New Faces, New Purpose

The band was in great demand! They had at least one request each week and had to sort out their schedules more and more. Of course, the ladies loved going all over the region, sharing the joy they had been given with others, so they were moving about in familiar places and some that even they had never really known.

When Janine tried to find the locations without one of the ladies with her, she would invariably get lost. Navigation was not her trustworthy attribute. She had usually relied upon John for that, and now she was the one discovering new places and new roads to get there.

In September they had been invited to go to a nursing home in a community about twenty miles to the north. No one had been there, but the directions were easy to follow, and they found themselves at a beautifully accommodated facility in which everything matched, from window dressings to lamps to flooring. An elevator took them to the third floor of Serenity

Home, where they were directed down a long hallway to a very large room that had previously been set up with round tables for the dining room.

Janine asked to have some of the tables moved away from one section for the band to have space to perform. All modification s were quickly taken care of, and soon the residents were brought in one by one. Each and every one was in a wheelchair, which surprised the ladies. They came in, and some did not so much as look up to see where they were. Some wore bibs and remained in a sleepy mode; others looked around and at the band members and smiled, but hardly realized that they were going to be entertained.

The band was being challenged to go where very few *would* go. To an Alzheimer unit! They had no idea that's what the Serenity Home was all about, and they knew that they had their work cut out for them. Janine went around to each and every person while the members of band set out their instruments in their assigned places for entertaining.

It wasn't long before Janine realized that she was speaking to people who would not respond. Since she had never been in a room with anyone of such dire straits, she was totally perplexed as to how to handle herself. She took a hand and said "Hello." The lady moved her body a bit but did not look up.

She came upon a man who was staring into space and tried to get into that space for communication. She said "Hello" and took his hand, and he gripped it so hard, she thought her bones would break. She looked around for help, and finally, one of the health workers came over to her and told her to relax her hand and rub his arm with her other. She did, and he released her hand and smiled. That was good.

She made a valiant attempt at meeting the residents, but didn't know if anyone knew she was there.

Eventually, she looked up, said a short prayer for help, turned to the band members, and started the music. All songs were performed as well as could be without any noticeable response for a while. As they began to sing a song or two that everyone should know, some patients smiled, lips moved, and seemingly, contact was made. The band never worked as hard as they did that day, doing all that they could to bring a smile and feeling of happiness to such a pitifully pathetic situation.

Janine noticed a very large woman who was probably no older than forty practically lying nearly flat on her back on a rolled bed. She seemed to be moving her lips with every song, but nothing really came forth. Janine was drawn to her and, after the performance, went to her and touched her and held her hands. She said, "Did you enjoy the music?"

Janine was shocked when she nodded slightly with a beautiful smile. "Dear God, thank you!" Janine said silently as she was overcome with gratitude for the precious gift of that smile.

"Did you sing?" she asked. She knew the totally disabled woman didn't sing out, but she seemed to be singing within.

The woman kept her lovely smile and nodded again. Janine almost cried with the realization of what the band could do. *So is this it? Is this why the Lord has called us?* She felt the nudge and knew.

There was much discussion from the ladies as they gathered together to go into the cars about how hard that was. They were exhausted. They did see that they definitely needed to go to places such as that, but nevertheless, since this was the first, they could not immediately rejoice.

Two weeks later, Janine received a telephone call from the social director of Serenity Home thanking her and the band for the wonderful afternoon her beloved residents enjoyed. She told Janine that they saw responses they hadn't seen in months from some who attended and that the band was a godsend.

Janine hung up the phone and outright cried. "Forgive me, Lord, for thinking that the band was simply fun for those who were in it. Of course, You have given all of us a joy beyond measure, but now that I realize why we are together, and that realization will help us to be of more help to others."

12

The Final Move

The Lord was leading. After the eye-opening gathering at the Serenity House, the band was contacted by several other nursing homes and assisted-living homes. They were very happy to be offered the opportunity to go where they were actually needed and could be of real service.

At the Hanover House, most of the people were on their own except for community meals in the dining room. The building was beautiful, and everyone who came to the entertainment was dressed very nicely. They led fairly normal lives, went shopping now and then; a lot of them went to church outside of the facility with church friends who came to pick them up. But they still needed some uplifting, and the band was just the conduit for that. Most of the residents were left alone after family members had passed and/or children had moved to another community. It was just the place for a pleasant environment with very little responsibilities. One could tell that they held sadness within them though. Who wouldn't be sad if you were nearly the last of your family and dear friends to survive?

Leaving the Hanover House, Iola said she probably would end up in one of those someday. That shocked everyone! Who could imagine Iola not being totally responsible for herself and making all her own decisions?

ᡣᡣᡣ

Later that evening, Iola thought again about how lovely the facility was and how nice for the residents who lived there, but she knew it wasn't what she wanted to do at this stage of her life. *I want to be a real part of church and a real part of the band. This is a good thing, and I do enjoy it. Maybe the day will come when I have to sell my house, but I hope not too soon.*

She lived in a big house, nicely positioned with a view. She needed a house like that when the boys were young, but as is with most people, she has no need for all the space anymore. Of course, she has her collections to fill the spaces. She collected beautiful bells, had several sets of fine china, nice linens that were hardly needed anymore, magazines from twenty years back, every church bulletin she had ever used, children's costumes and so much more. Do all old ladies have collections? They do, and that's a problem. They piled up in corners, closets, and drawers and were extremely difficult to throw away or hand over to Goodwill because most assumed their collections and items of interest would also be important to someone in the family some day. But the probability was that others would not share in their interests, but would have ideas and collections of their own, which of course will resume the cycle in years to come.

One of Iola's constant reminders was that she didn't have much hair anymore. It was dreadful! *I can't hear and I can't hair! Ha-ha!* Well, it wasn't very laughable in all truth. She knew of some women who wore wigs and had decided to go see about getting fitted for one. *People will think I've lost my mind or flipped my wig if I do that. So what? I like to look nice, and it is getting more and more impossible to comb over the bald spots.*

The Hanover House brought a lot of reality into the lives of each member of the band, and it really caused them to be even more grateful for the lives they still had. Yes, for the most part, each and every one—except Anne—now lived alone and could go to a facility like that and be around others and communicate and interact more. They say that interaction helped to make each day better, and it's true. But the ladies were interacting and keeping their minds working and their bodies moving and so were being held off a while from the near-final fate of selling and moving.

13

Front-Page News

"We're coming up to the holidays of Thanksgiving and Christmas. I'm thinking we might take some time off during this period. What do you think?" Janine asked.

"I don't have anything else to do," was Julia's quick answer. Of course, she didn't. Her children were living away and she had absolutely no family in the area. She enjoyed church, piano lessons, but nothing else.

"I like going out and about during the holidays," said Pauline.

"What else is there? Sit at home and watch television as we always have done?" said Bea.

"Yes, but think of Janine here," Anne said. "She does have a family and babies coming too. She'll be working hard at the church with extra music and pageants. I also think we should pause over the holidays. I'll be getting some company."

Janine assured them that she could handle it all, even though she knew she would be stretching both ends to do so.

Pauline said she did have a new request and maybe they should consider it. It was a retired ministers' Christmas party.

That sounded intriguing to everyone but also a little intimidating to be entertaining the *saints of the church.* However, it was a consensus that they could go. The gathering would be within a few miles of West Hope, so they wouldn't have to travel far in the cold.

So it was agreed: the retired ministers and nothing more until perhaps March or April.

No one liked the thought of not continuing steadily, but it was true that they couldn't just go dragging themselves out in bad weather, and if they planned anything and the weather took a turn for the worse, it would have to be cancelled.

The day of the ministers' luncheon was a beautiful December day. The ladies were up to the mark with their songs and dancing. Janine had prepared a list of Christmas carols as a sing-along, which worked well, and it was a great day. The ladies wore Christmas blouses and jewelry and each had a Santa hat to wear during the sing-along.

They received many compliments afterward, and a person from one of the major Pittsburgh newspapers wanted to do an article about the band.

That article was the catalyst to something no one could have imagined!

The reporter apparently had a lot of influence at the newspaper because the article about the band was on the front page of the Lifetime section in a Sunday edition. It took up nearly the entire page and told all about the band with pictures.

The phones were ringing off the hooks. This was definitely part of The Plan, if ever there was one. *This band is going places whether we like it or not. It is just meant to be.* Janine was getting nervous considering the possibilities. She brushed it all aside and decided not to get into making any plans for the band until after the babies were here.

But the phone kept ringing. "Can we have the band for our function? Are you available for Valentine's Day? Can your band come for our senior party in March? Could you come to our Women's Day function at the regional level? The Homemakers of the State of West Virginia would like to have the band entertain." *What? How far do we want to go?*

Janine's answer to all was that they do not go out in the wintertime. She would be happy to discuss entertainments from April throughout the warm weather, so some of those who called were being booked ahead.

14

The Traditional Christmas Eve

Right now, it's Christmas, and the concert is nearly ready, and music, music, music is on Janine's plate and stacking up along with decorating the house, baking cookies, and looking forward to a little rest.

Isn't this just what I was doing in Innesport? I thought I was getting away from being rushed and having no time for myself. Yes, that's true, but this really is different. Who isn't busy at Christmas anyway? It's the season to enjoy all that is involved with welcoming the Christ Child and I love it!

Deborah was coming to a place where she could hardly function on her own. Dr. Doloria has suggested that plans be put in place for her period of seclusion and rest.

Kathy called her mother.

"Hi, I'm really concerned for Debbie. She needs to get off of her feet. Can you believe how large she is? I don't know how much longer she can walk around, actually."

"I know. I offered for her to come here after Christmas, but she thinks it would be too much for me. I believe we'd be fine. What do you think?"

"Well, she may be right, but I would be happy to come over and lend a hand, though. I'd have her with us if only the extra bed wasn't up that big flight of stairs. I don't want her to go be in a hospital bed for a couple of months. Gee whiz! We can care for her. Let's think on it some more."

Janine talked with John. He absolutely wanted Debbie to be with her mother. Of course! There was really no question about it. Janine was perfectly satisfied that Debbie should come home, so to speak. They would enjoy each another, and Janine's motherly instincts were beginning to respond in full force.

The family was smaller at Christmas Eve services, as Debbie could not sit on a pew. She and Robert would meet up with them after church at the home place and sing carols and eat cookies as usual. Somehow, Janine finished all seasonal responsibilities without collapsing and was happy and bright throughout.

No snow.

"Thank goodness it isn't snowing," Janine said. "I'd be so disappointed if Deborah couldn't come for Christmas Eve," Janine said to John.

"Me too. When are we going to move her in? Isn't it time?"

"I think it's past time, but everyone was kind of putting it off while I finished up tonight. It won't take us any time to get her a room ready. There's really nothing to do. She could pack up some stuff and stay tonight if she wanted to, but for some reason, she and Robert wanted to spend the night together. That's fine. When she's ready . . ."

The Langs went home after Christmas Eve services and picked up Prince. After all, he loved family get-togethers as much as the people did.

They're back! I knew they would be home soon. I've been looking and waiting a while.

"Here he is! Hello, Prince. Would you like to go to Grandma's?" Greg asked, knowing full well that Prince would jump at the chance.

Yes. Yes. He began circling around the large room, puffing in excitement.

"Come on, then. Let's go!"

He jumped into the backseat with the girls, practically taking up the full seat for himself. The girls giggled and loved on him. He was one very lucky dog. He knew it too. He had the best family in the world.

They were back just as Janine and John put out the cookies and punch, so everyone was in the kitchen enjoying the results of Janine's specialties.

Who's here? Prince heard the car door.

"Prince, come here. Do not jump on Debbie. Come on, stay here in the kitchen." Kathy was very concerned he might knock her off balance, which surely would be easy to do these days.

Prince did as he was told, but it wasn't easy.

The family left him there and met Deborah and Robert at the door. God bless her. She needed assistance, and her coat didn't cover her at all! She was smiling anyway. Nothing could steal away her joy and happiness. She believed it was all going to be worth it in the end and didn't concentrate on today's misery.

"I'm looking to the days ahead," she always told everyone, and she had the stamina to do just that. She actually loved being pregnant and talking to her babies. It was a great feeling.

Prince was beginning to bark. He wanted to see Deborah. After she was seated in the high-standing Empire chair, Kathy called Prince to come on in.

Yay! Deborah is here. I want to find her secret.

He went straight to her. She could hardly bend over far enough to pet him, but he just wanted to be near to her, so that was fine with him. He sat and placed his head on her lap. She really didn't have much of a lap, and the family laughed at his meager attempt. He stayed put anyway because the secret was so very close. Everyone settled in.

The tree was beautiful and full of many ornaments that brought back memories to the family. Some were made by Kathy, Debbie, and Harry when they were children, and some given as gifts from Karen, Meghan, and the boy cousins in Oklahoma. There was a pickle hidden on the tree, and no one was permitted to be near to the tree until a signal was given to visually inspect for it. It was all part of the tradition, and everyone appreciated the long-standing customs.

Grandma and Granddad presented everyone with one Christmas gift, another tradition in the family for Christmas Eve. The next would be the singing of Carols as Grandma or one of the girls played the piano. Tears welled up in Janine's eyes as she appreciated so much the love of the family and the joy of following through each year with the comfort of consistency.

"Hark! The herald angels sing, 'Glory to the newborn King,'" they sang.

When they sang "Gentle Mary Laid Her Child" and "Away in a Manger," Deborah was unconsciously rocking her babies.

They began to discuss the difficulty that Mary must have felt on the road to Bethlehem, being so full of child, as they looked at Deb. She said she must have been very frightened to not find a place to lay her baby as the birth pangs were coming on.

"It was all in God's hands," John said. "He had a plan—a perfect plan. The Holy Family was blessed, and so are we."

"Yes. We should remember the Blessed Mother who accepted without hesitation the task before her," said Janine.

"Let's sing 'Silent Night,'" Kathy suggested, which of course had to be sung on Christmas Eve. The babies were comforted, apparently, by the song and were still as the night itself; and the family should have left it at that, but they added "Joy to the World" to the repertoire, and those babies started to dance! Prince backed up. *Is Deborah all right?* he wondered?

"Good grief! The babies either loved the song or would have preferred to rock through 'Silent Night,' because they are really excited right now!" She wiggled around trying to find a comfortable way to sit but that took a while.

Prince edged back over and once again put his head on Deborah's lap. His ears were perked though. *The secret is here, but I can't see it!*

John was concerned for his daughter.

"Let's settle up when you are going to come here, Deb. We're ready anytime, and I think you should be getting off your feet as Dr. Doloria said."

"I'm ready. How about January 2? Would that be okay?"

"Of course," Janine and John both agreed.

Robert seemed relieved that a date had been set and was happy that they moved to a house near John and Janine. He was grateful that they wanted to help them in the present situation. Being a physician himself, he knew that Deb was under stress.

The rest of the evening went beautifully. They discussed everything about the future—the babies, the nursery, Harry, Rhonda and the boys in Oklahoma—and in general, their many blessings.

Debbie and Robert left first, and everyone was helpful as they could be.

The rest were gone without hesitation because Santa was soon to arrive at the Langs' and they needed to get bedded down. Suddenly, the house was empty!

"The house is so quiet," Janine said.

"I know."

"Santa doesn't need to come here. We have everything we could possibly need or want," Janine said. She was not tired anymore. Everything had been accomplished, and she could look ahead to Deborah and the babies being with them. It would be a good and satisfying experience.

"Merry Christmas, honey," John said as he reached out his open arms to her. The years shared together flashed by as they held on once again.

"Merry Christmas," she said. They walked through the house and turned out most of the lights. They always left one lit to light the way for the Christ Child. They stood before the light. John said, "Thank you, Father, for giving us the Light of the World."

They slept cuddled together and woke to a glorious new day, rested and at peace.

15

Miracles Happen

During the next weeks, Janine and John were very happy to have Deborah in their home day and night. It eased their minds greatly to know every minute of each day that she was comfortable and doing well. Janine hustled about cooking, caring for her daughter, and reverting to being a mother for a short time once again.

Deborah was unbelievably large. Her babies were growing, and there didn't seem to be another microinch to be found to hold them. Deb seemed to be stretched to the limit physically, but spiritually and mentally, she was adjusting to her pregnancy well. Janine admired her tenacity and ability to be joyful under all circumstances, which brought sunshine into her every day, and into the lives of all those who in the home. John and Janine were constantly smiling and counting their blessings throughout the days.

Robert took Deborah to her appointments each week and always gave the same response: she's doing well; the babies are doing well. Keep on keeping on. It won't be long.

January turned into February, and the skies seemed a little bluer.

February is a wonderful little month. It is short and promises us love from all corners. It also promises that spring is approaching. Hearts and flowers appear everywhere and thoughts clearly move away from the bleakness of the weather to love, hope, and anticipation.

As Janine pondered these thoughts, the telephone rang.

"Mrs. Stephens, this is Charlie Harris, the program director of FBN's Saturday night show, *Miracles Happen.* I have seen the AP release of the article concerning The Band of Hope that was written for publication originally in the *Pittsburgh Daily Outreach* recently. It is the hope of our programming committee that we might be able to have The Band of Hope come to New York City where we could do a story about your mission and have the band perform for a national audience."

Janine was aghast and nearly speechless.

"Mr. Harris, this is so unexpected that I don't know what to say. Are you serious?"

"Yes, believe me, I am. I can certainly understand your apprehension. I would suggest that we meet together with certain knowledgeable people whom we both know so that you can be assured that I am on the up-and-up."

"Even so . . ."

"Mrs. Stephens, would you be comfortable sitting down with your minister and the senior executive of your church district? Have you met her?"

"Actually yes, I do know Ruth Reimer. We were both on the same docket earlier last year."

"Well, believe me, I know her as well and would be happy to set up a meeting together sometime soon in Pittsburgh. I'm not surprised that you are uncomfortable with a complete stranger calling you like this, but I had to start somewhere."

"I think we could meet; however, let me discuss this with my husband before I talk with anyone. Could you call me back at say 7:00 p.m. tomorrow?"

"I'll do that. Keep in mind that we have a wide audience. I feel sure that many would benefit from the story of your ladies and the band. Our mission at Faith Broadcasting Network is to spread the Gospel of Christ throughout the world. We have had many struggles over the years, growing into a major network, but our faith has never wavered. I sense that you are a strong proponent of the Gospel and have a great mission yourself. We would work together for good and we will pay all the travel expenses and lodging as well."

"I'm still not sure I believe this, but I will talk with my husband and minister, and have an answer for you tomorrow, I hope."

"Thank you, Mrs. Stephens. I'll be eager to speak with you again."

"Yes, thank you. Good-bye."

"Good-bye."

16

To Be or Not to Be?

Janine walked into her bedroom and sat on the bedside chair for a long time. Her mind was whirling in every direction. *Surely, this is not the Lord's planning. I'm working with elderly ladies, and I'm not young myself. A trip to New York City? I can't even think straight. Oh my!*

She decided after a while that this was not the Lord's idea at all but just a crazy notion that could not work in any way, shape, or form. *Yes, that's it. I'll not even mention it to John. I'll wait for this Mr. Harris to call tomorrow, and I'll just tell him I have personally made the decision not to pursue it at all because it is not something that can be accomplished.*

We can't just pack up a group of elderly women and all the equipment and run off to the big city without some sort of failures or consequences that we would not even be able to predict. I can't be responsible for all of us. This is just too much.

What if someone falls? What if someone gets sick? And then who is going to carry all the stuff we have?

Well, that settles it. We can't do it. That's that.

She was too rattled and flustered to move. She just sat there and stared into space.

"Mom."

It was Deborah in the other room.

"Honey, are you all right?"

"Yes, I'm fine. I just wondered if I might have some more water, if you don't mind."

"Sure, of course. I'll go get you some."

Janine's hands were trembling. She decided to try to get the telephone call out of her mind if possible. After all, her daughter was in the final weeks or days of her pregnancy. Deborah could actually go into labor, and Dr. Deloria had recommended complete bed rest, which was what she was attempting to do with the help of her parents.

All was ready, and everyone was on call. No one wanted to miss a minute of anything that was happening.

"Thanks, Mom. I try to keep hydrated. You are a gem."

"Deborah, I am so happy to have you right here where I can be sure you are fine every minute of the day and night. It is good for me and your father as well. If you weren't here, John would have us driving over to your house all the time."

"I know. It's wonderful and all for the best. Robert and I hope to be as good at being parents as you and Dad have always been."

"Well, thank you. You and Robert will be wonderful parents. Do you want anything else? Do you need to go to the bathroom before you try to get some sleep?"

"No, I don't think so. I really feel pretty well today. The babies have calmed down a bit. I think I'll get right off to sleep. Thanks for the warming pillow. It sure is comforting."

"You're welcome, honey. Ring this bell if you need us. I'll be right next door."

"Okay, Mom. Goodnight."

"Goodnight, sweetie."

17

Whose Apple Is This?

Janine walked back into the kitchen after leaving Deborah for the night, and John confronted her.

"What was that telephone call you received earlier? You haven't said a word about it."

"Oh, it was just some crazy person talking to me about the Kitchen Band."

"Crazy? I don't like the sound of that."

"No, not crazy. I'm sorry. He was very nice, really. He wanted to talk with me about the band doing something, but I don't think it will work out."

Her decision of not telling John about the call was fizzling out. She wants to discuss it with him as she does all things. This was very hard for Janine, but she is trying to stick to her decision.

"I think I'll just go get ready for bed."

"Hey, hey, wait a minute here. I can see you are trying to hide something from me. That's not like you. Are you sure you don't want to talk about it?"

At that, Janine began to struggle against crying. John could see her tears forming, and he went to her and put his arms around her and held her while she actually burst into tears.

"I didn't want to tell you about the call because I'm kind of upset and need to sort it out. I don't know if I want you to get involved with this."

"What? If you're upset, I want to know why."

"Well, it's something that could be wonderful or it could be wrong. I have to decide which it is really. I should probably not try to figure it out right now but wait until morning."

Now he was troubled. What to do?

"Janine, we can usually work things out pretty well together. Two heads are better than one, you know."

"Okay, I'll tell you."

"John, I know this is going to sound ridiculous. Here's the thing: I've been offered a bite out of an apple. On the surface it looks pretty ripe and sweet. I'm afraid of it, actually."

She told him nearly word-for-word the conversation she had with Mr. Harris. She walked around the kitchen, stopping a few times to reiterate what she had just said. The more she talked, the calmer she became because she knew that John truly cared for her and would want to help.

When she finished explaining, he said, "I think you should go ahead and talk with Pastor Dan tomorrow if you can and see what he thinks. It sounds like a giant undertaking, yet if it is God's will, it will all work out. Quite honestly, I'm shocked, and yet we shouldn't be surprised, considering the way this has all worked out until now. Maybe this is where it's supposed to go.

But I'll tell you this, only God knows the answer, and we'd better take it to Him before you go any further."

She thought, *Of course, he's right. Everything has been directed by Him all along. Is this part of His plan for us? I need to know for sure.* "What's wrong with me? I know better than to jump to conclusions now more than ever."

He took her hands in his, and they bowed together in prayer, trusting in the Lord to give them the answer. Without knowing for sure at the moment the prayer ended, they both decided that the Lord would answer in His own time and they would then know. Janine felt relief and peace, and they both slept well during the night.

Janine jumped up the next morning and went in to check on Deborah, who was smiling and happy and said she was doing just fine, so Janine went to the kitchen to start the day with breakfast for everyone.

Later she called Pastor Dan, and they decided to meet with Mr. Harris and Ruth Reimer sometime in the near future. Pastor Dan didn't seem to be worried about the offer and told Janine that the truth will arise and whatever turns up will be right. She felt fine about that and decided to continue with the conversation with Mr. Harris that evening.

In the meantime, she knew that she would have time to make the decision later. She had many things to do at the house, and she liked working with her hands to rest her mind.

The Christmas ornaments were still not in the boxes, wreaths were still hanging, and there were other items to put away. Between checking with Deborah and handling the seasonal transition, she managed the day very well.

Robert came to the house for dinner as expected and was still visiting with Deborah when the telephone call came in from Mr. Harris.

Janine quickly picked up the telephone and escaped into her bedroom to have a conversation with him. He seemed like such a good and honest man, and she had no difficulty in working with him to set up the time for Pastor Dan, Ruth Reimer, and herself to meet together with him in the near future.

That was that! She could calmly leave it for a time while she took care of Deborah, arranged choral music, planned choir practices, and glanced into the future as best she could. The time for a real decision about the New York trip would come later.

18

Adele

Adele Marsh had been to the cardiologist, arranged by her personal physician, due to some palpitations and general ill feelings during the past few months. She didn't want to tell her grandson, Billie, about her present situation—not until she knew for sure what the diagnosis would be. She and Billie were very close. He was a wonderful person, taking care of his mother, Candice, for years. Candice had been disabled for a long, long time from an automobile accident, and Billie never wavered in his devotion to her. Now that Billie was married, he took complete responsibility for his mother.

Adele was so very happy to know that Candice would be in Billie's hands in the future, because she was beginning to recognize that her health was not what it used to be. She had not mentioned to Bea, her closest friend, that she was not feeling well. She wouldn't keep it from her. She would tell her soon.

Adele never saw the cardiologist. She passed from this world in her sleep. When Billie couldn't reach her by telephone, he went to her house and found her in bed with a smile on her face. Everyone said that most likely she saw Jesus because she was so close to Him throughout her earthly days.

Bea called Janine. She was crying.

"Bea, what's wrong?" Janine asked.

"Oh, it's awful, just awful. Adele has died."

"What?"

"Yes, Adele. She died last night. Billie found her in bed. I didn't know anything was wrong with her. She seemed to have some discomfort of some kind but never talked about it. Oh, I'm just sick over this. She was my best friend."

"Oh, Bea, I'm so sorry. Would you like for me to come up?"

"Yes, I really would."

"Does Pastor Dan know?"

"Yes, he does. Billie called him first."

"I'll be there as soon as I can."

"Okay. Thanks."

Janine was crying too when John walked into the room. She told him about Adele. They were shocked. It was difficult to believe that it happened.

What a loss! She was the most spiritual member of the Kitchen Band. The band looked to her for strength and comfort all the time. She was truly a wonderful person.

John let Janine go on to Bea's house. She had a cell phone for contact in case Deborah needed her, but John would be at home the entire time.

When Janine arrived at Bea's house, she found her deep in her sorrow. How sad to see her like that—she was always so joyful in Janine's presence. Janine let her talk about her good friend, shared tears together, and comforted each other for an hour at least.

By the time Janine had left, Pastor Dan had stopped by to tell them the arrangements and prayed with them also.

It was beginning to blow up a real snowstorm, and Pastor Dan advised Janine to get on home before it piled up into complete misery. She left, feeling the great loss of her dear friend and sorrow for Bea and the other members of band who would also feel the terrible loss this day.

Tears welled up often on her trip back home. The roads were getting slick and she knew that John would be worried about her. She pulled off of the road and called him to tell him she was on her way. He was uncomfortable with the weather situation and asked her to please be very careful. The wind had picked up and she could hardly see out of the rear and side windows to get back onto the road.

She took a deep breath, asked the Lord for help, and pulled out just as a large truck came upon her. She swerved to the right and skidded just as the truck passed by. It took her quite a while to catch her breath when she recognized that she had barely escaped being run down by that big truck. She knew also that it was a blessing from the Lord and not just luck that was on her side.

She didn't know whether or not to continue toward home or to call John to come and get her. She sat really still. What to do? She didn't want John to leave Deborah. She didn't want John on the road either. She was afraid to drive herself. She finally decided she would drive herself home and prayed that the Lord would stay with her and keep her safe along the way. Praying all the while, she came to her driveway, saw all the lights on in the house and on the porch, and pulled into the garage. She finally took in a deep breath. The Lord was with her, and she made it safely home.

She was silently singing her beloved prayer of Saint Patrick, "Christ Be with Me," as she turned off the engine, and her dear husband, John, opened the car door for her.

Janine had made it safely home. It crossed her mind that so had Adele.

19

Good-Bye and Hello

The members of the band all gathered together at the funeral home and stayed together for a couple of hours. They were a comfort to one another as they told stories about Adele and of her goodness. No one doubted that she was one of God's own.

Billie brought his mother, Constance, and everyone felt so sorry for her. She was devastated over the death of her mother, who had loved her and cared for her for many, many years. Death was a reckoning time—a time to sum up the value of a life—and everyone counted Adele's life as more valuable than gold, and she was one who would be missed as a precious friend.

The friends attended the funeral and stayed for the dinner prepared by Hope Church. They had all prepared a dish to take as was the custom. Janine also took a salad and appreciated the opportunity to play the organ for the service. She always said it was something she could give that she hoped would be helpful to the friends and family.

As the members of the band gathered together at one of the tables, the most frequent comment was that they never expected Adele to be the first to go. Of course, who could know these things? Someone said, "Live well, always do your best, and let God take care of the big things. Maybe someday we'll all understand."

ϒϒϒ

Mr. Harris called Janine a few days after the sad event, and Janine told him of their loss. He offered his condolences and said that they would be taking a few weeks to get together with the pastor and Ruth. He suggested a date, and she agreed only if she felt she could get away due to the upcoming birth.

"That will be no problem. We'll have lots of time to work out all the logistics of this project. We can actually have the trip scheduled for one of the summer months, if you think that would be best."

"Thank you very much for that suggestion. I really don't know if the ladies would even consider such a venture, and since we just lost one of our own, we'll have to wait a while to approach them about it."

"I totally understand. We'll see what we think when we get together soon. And again, I'm sorry for your loss. We'll be in touch."

She turned from the telephone and immediately went in to see Deborah who was totally miserable that morning and early afternoon.

"How are you feeling?"

"Oh dear. I feel absolutely washed out and yucky," she said. "Robert has called the doctor, and she wants me to go in to have her check me over. She said not to be surprised if she sends me to the hospital."

"I wouldn't be surprised, honey. My goodness. I never had such a load to carry and I was so uncomfortable and some days miserable too. You are far enough along now for the babies to be born, so she may decide enough is enough. I'd like to go with you, but perhaps it's best for you and Robert to share this moment alone together."

"I think that's right. No offense. You always understand."

"Well, I try to. I put myself in your position, and then I think what I would like. It's easy."

Robert came within no time of the conversation, and they both did their best to get Deborah dressed warm enough to get out of the house.

"Maybe we should have called the ambulance. The weather is horrendous out there. We still can."

He looked at John questioningly, and John said, "Go for it."

"Right."

The E-car was there within minutes and was prepared to take care of any emergency. Robert drove right behind and called Janine and John when they had all arrived safely to the doctor's office, which was conveniently located in the hospital.

The Stephens relaxed a bit then, except Janine who was always looking for opportunities. She leaped in and changed the bed sheets and freshened up the room for Deborah's return.

The telephone rang, and both John and Janine jumped for it. John won.

"John, she's going to stay at least the night. Dr. Doloria wants some tests run and wants to monitor her during the night. We're not looking at a C-section or inducing labor, so just relax and get a good night's sleep. I'll call you in the morning. I'll be staying here with her."

"That sounds like the right plan, Robert. Thanks for the call."

When he hung up, they both were happy that Deborah was in good hands, turned out the lights, and decided on getting as much sleep as possible.

That was the best thing they could do because at 7:30 a.m., Robert was on the phone again, saying that she had gone into labor!

They hurried through the necessary things, grabbed coats, scarves, gloves, boots, and left the house for the hospital. On the way, they called Kathy and also Harry in Oklahoma.

Everyone was ready, excited, and looking forward to welcoming the twins into the family.

Janine waited for John to park the car, and they walked into the hospital together. When they arrived at the proper floor and went to the waiting room, the receptionist asked them who they were looking for, and immediately they were whisked into another smaller room. There was no one in the room when they entered, but very soon after, someone came in and again asked who they were. When they found out that John and Janine were Deborah's parents, they sent word into the delivery room that they had arrived and came back to tell them that Deborah is at that moment birthing Baby A. The attendant left them and the grandparents were all alone with their thoughts. It seemed like an eternity, but it had only been about eight minutes when the attendant returned to tell them that Baby A had been born.

It was strange that Robert couldn't come out or the doctor, but in this case both were very involved with the life and transition of Baby B. Was Baby A fine? There really wasn't a word about that. The attendant left them again.

John and Janine sat down and held hands and waited.

No one returned.

Kathy came rushing through the outer door, out of breath, and hoping to be there in time.

Apparently she was, but no one could say for sure. She couldn't sit down but instead began to pace back and forth.

"What on earth is happening?" Janine asked.

"Well, when little Baby B came, they had a lot to do, and there wasn't anyone available to come out, I suppose," said John.

"That's ridiculous. Surely someone can look in and say everything's fine," said Kathy.

"What if it's not?" asked Janine.

"Now, Janine. Don't even think that way. No sense in worrying about something you don't even know about for sure," said John.

"I know how Mom feels," said Kathy. "Good grief! Please! Someone look in here!"

"I read where sometimes the second baby turns breech and then they have to do a C-section," Janine said.

"That's true," said Kathy. "But look at it this way: they are in the best place possible if that has happened."

Still there has been no word.

Janine's cell phone began to ring! That noise in the midst of them nearly caused heart attacks. Janine looked down. It was Harry.

"Hello, Harry."

"Mom, what's going on? We're waiting for someone to tell us something. Is Deb all right?"

"Yes, I think so. We are sitting here in the waiting room, but we don't know enough to tell you. The first baby was born, but we don't know her condition. We are assuming that the second little girl is here also because there cannot be much time between births or there could be extreme trauma to the second baby. So hopefully everything is good and someone will come out soon and tell us. Wait! Here is someone right now."

It was Dr. Deloria. Thank goodness!

"Mr. and Mrs. Stephens and—Kathy, right?"

"Yes."

"I'm sorry you had to wait so long for word of your little granddaughters. The first little one came in a hurry but the second was turning from breech to vertex, and we gave her the chance to do so rather than rush into doing a C-section. The wait was worth it as she was born with an ideal delivery. So we have two perfect and identical twin girls. They were definitely monozygotic—identical in all respects, sharing the same placenta. I'm sure Robert will tear himself away in time."

They all smiled knowing how thrilled Robert would be.

"Harry, Harry. Are you still there?"

"Yes."

"Oh, my goodness, I forgot I had you on the line. But since I do, did you hear all that was going on?"

"Pretty much so. I guess I'm Uncle Harry to two more precious little girls, right?"

"Looks that way. Do you want me to put you on speaker phone and keep you on for a while?"

"Sure."

"Okay. Oh, here comes Robert!"

"Hey, everyone, she did fantastic, absolutely fantastic! And I have the most beautiful little baby girls ever. No offense, Kathy. But you know how I feel, right?"

"Yes, Robert, of course I do. And I'm sure you do have absolutely beautiful little baby girls."

Janine went over to give him a hug, and she could feel his heart beating through all the clothing. He looked so happy and excited.

John reached out and, in the manly fashion, shook hands with the new father.

"There's nothing like being a father to put you in your place, Robert. But it's a good place, believe me," John remarked.

"We'll be able to take you to the room in just a bit. One weighed five pounds and six ounces, and the other five pounds and seven ounces. Big babies. Big babies—my goodness, how did she do it?" Robert was amazed even though as a doctor he had seen many new babies and perhaps new births, but this was Deborah!

"We are so happy for you and Debbie, Robert. Having children changes a lot of things, but it is really worth anything you have to do," Janine said.

"I'm sure. I can't wait to get started. I'm so glad they are not really small, and that now we can take them home with us."

"Dr. Franklin, we have the room ready," the attendant announced.

"Oh, thank you. I must tell you, there is a sterile wall unit that you can use as you enter. It is hospital policy, and we approve that as well."

"Of course, no problem," said John.

Robert led them in, and there was Deborah, holding a baby in each arm, smiling a smile that couldn't even be described.

"Look what I have," she said.

The four followed Robert to her bedside and marveled at the beautiful babies. Of course, Janine and Kathy had to shed a tear or two of gratitude, and John wiped his eyes before anyone noticed.

"Mom, Dad, Kathy, meet Annette and Annabelle."

They all three loved the French names that they had chosen. They just stared at the babies and wondered if there would ever be a time when they could tell them apart.

"Harry, Harry, are you there?"

"Yes, put me on the phone with my sister."

"We'll have to keep you on speaker phone. She has her hands full at the moment."

"I guess so. Deb, I'm so happy for you, and the boys can't wait to meet their new cousins. Congratulations, sis, and good job!"

"Thanks, Harry. You'll have to bring the boys around really soon so they can see them while they are so little. This is amazing!"

"We will really try to get there soon, I promise. In the meantime, keep them healthy and happy and tell them their uncle Harry already loves them."

"I will. Thank you, Harry."

Well, the accolades went on and on. Kathy called the girls who were home for a snow day, and they got to congratulate Aunt Deb. Even Prince was barking something no one could understand. Uncle Greg had gone to work, but he knew and had expressed to Kathy his joy for the family.

Everyone could see that Deb was getting tired. Dr. Deloria had ordered her to get some rest and to stay overnight at least one night and perhaps more. Time would tell. In the meantime, the family would leave the new parents to themselves and let them revel in their joy.

Everyone needs to have a spark ignited in their lives now and then, and nothing did it any better than a baby—or two. "Pretty two-rific," as John would say.

20

Little Jimmy

The snow lingered on, built up a little more, and drifted as very strong winds blew in through the region. Most people stayed inside and kept warm. Iola was certainly one of them. She had no intention of moving out of the house on a day such as this. *It feels like it's below zero out there.* She knew it wasn't, but she layered on the clothing and made a nice hot cup of tea and curled up with a book.

Iola didn't hear well without her hearing aid, and she didn't hear little Jimmy Adams at the side door until he had nearly given up that she might answer his knock.

She picked up her hearing aid and listened. *That's someone at the door.*

She walked to the door and opened it just as she had put her hearing aid back in.

"Hello, Mrs. MacCowan. I was wondering if you would like to have your sidewalk shoveled off. Mr. Gordon gave me this nice shovel yesterday when I was over his way, so I can do a nice job for you."

"Oh, Jimmy. Step in for a minute. You must be freezing."

"No, I'm fine, really."

"Do you have a scarf?"

"Nope, never had one."

"Well, wait here. I'm going to give you one. It used to belong to one of my sons. It will only take a minute or two."

She came back carrying a fine wool scarf and wrapped it around his neck. He had a ragged toboggan on his head, but she couldn't remember if she had anything to replace that.

"I would like for you to go ahead with the sidewalks over to the driveway if you want to. When you get finished, I'll have some good warm hot chocolate for you."

"Oh gee, Mrs. MacCowan, that sure would be nice."

He turned into the wind and began to shovel the snow.

God bless him. Considering his home life, he is still a nice young fellow.

Iola made a quick telephone call to Julia and asked her if she would like for little Jimmy to stop by and shovel for her, and Julia was very happy to have him do it for a number of reasons.

"I'll send him over your way."

She started getting the hot chocolate ready, got out two cups, a plate for cookies, and looked outside to see how he was doing just as he was returning to the house.

"Come on in. I have hot chocolate ready for you. We'll just sit down and enjoy some together. Mrs. Gillanders would like for you to shovel her walk too. I told her I would send you on over there. I hope that's okay with you."

Jimmy smiled. "Oh yes, ma'am. That's good. I'm hopin' to keep as busy as I can today."

"How is your mother, Jimmy?"

"Not very good. I'm scared she might not get well. She went to the hospital a couple of days ago, and we ain't heard nothin' at all."

As a very strict school teacher, it was all Iola could do not to correct his grammar.

"I'm so sorry. Is your sister all right?"

"Yes. She takes care of me right fine. She can cook when we have food enough for her to do it."

Iola's heart jumped with sadness hearing those words.

"Where is your father?"

"Well, nobody knows. He just up and ran out one day, and that was that."

"So it's just you and Sally at home right now?"

"Yes."

Iola was so troubled with the situation that her mind was whirling about what could be done to help that family and how she could find out about the mother's condition. She'd find out. She would not rest until she did.

Jimmy drank the chocolate milk and ate several cookies. At that point, Iola was wondering when the last time he actually ate anything was.

When he finished, he hurriedly put his coat and scarf on and seemed eager to get going.

"I'll go see Mrs. Gillander right away."

"Here, Jimmy, is some money for the fine shoveling job. Can you come back tomorrow and check and see if I need any more work done?"

It was the only thing she could think of saying. Maybe by tomorrow she would figure out what could be done about Jimmy and Sally.

"Thank you, Mrs. MacCowan. I'll try to stop by tomorrow."

"Good. I'll look for you maybe around two o'clock in the afternoon or if there is school, right after school, okay?"

"Yes, that's okay with me."

"Well, I'd better go. Thanks."

And with that he was gone. But he left something behind: Iola with a job to do.

ᕗᕗᕗ

Julia recognized that Jimmy needed warmth and comforting. She asked him to come inside after he finished the small job of a short sidewalk, the porch, and steps.

"Jimmy, is everything okay at home?"

"No. My mother is in the hospital, my father has left us, and Sally and I are alone right now. Sally can cook and do dishes, and I chopped a lot of wood, so we keep the living room warm with the wood stove. We just sleep in there when it's cold like this. But I'm scared that my mother will not come home. We have not heard a single word about her in days."

"Oh my goodness, dear. I'm so sorry. Do you know what? I made a big pot of soup yesterday, and I'd like for you to take some of that with you. I wondered what I'd do with it all."

"Well, that sure is a nice offer. I guess Sally would like that. I would too. Thank you very much."

"You are welcome. And here is some money for your work. You are a fine shoveler."

"Thank you. I'm going to stop at the Country Store and get us some apples and bread and milk. Now that I have earned some money, I can do it."

"Well, that's a fine young lad, Jimmy. You are doing just what is right to do. I'm very proud of you."

"Thank you."

"Now wait here, and I'll put some soup in a nice big container for you."

Julia went into the kitchen and was almost crying, thinking of these dear children and the life they were leading. *What else can I do to help?*

For now she hoped that the soup would help. She might come up with something else later.

"Jimmy, I'm sure glad you stopped by today. Any time it snows, please come and help me out, will you?"

"Yes, ma'am, I will. And thanks for the soup. It sure smells good, and Sally is going to be so happy tonight."

When Jimmy left, Julia called Iola.

"Hello, Iola. Did you talk with Jimmy?"

"Yes, I did. I'm so disturbed about his home situation. Did he tell you his father has left?"

"Yes, and his mother is in the hospital!"

"Yes. I can't think of anything but try to figure out what we can do to help."

"I want to help. I'm too old to go tramping out in this weather and climbing that hill to his house, or I would go up there and help out. But on the other hand, they probably wouldn't like that either. Who do we know besides us older folks who would know what to do?"

"I was thinking of Pastor Dan," said Iola.

"That's a great idea. Yes, he would know exactly what to do and do it too. I sent some soup with Jimmy. I'm thinking that some of us can provide some meals. Maybe Bea and Rachael might want to divvy in. Actually, if the church were made aware of this, there could be more done, I'd guess."

"You are right on track, Julia. Absolutely. That's what we must do. I can call Pastor Dan if you want me to, or you can."

"No, you do it. You are better with words than I am."

"I can do that. I will. I'll call him right away. He might even go to the hospital and find out what more he can about Mrs. Adams too."

"Well, that feels better. I was so shook up over this dear little guy, I never would have been able to rest until I knew that something was happening in his favor."

"Right, I agree. I told Jimmy to come back tomorrow and see if I had any more work for him to do. In the meantime, I'm going to look for a good knit cap for his head. You know, my boys left stuff behind. I can dig in some drawers and will probably find one at least. Maybe even one for Sally. People like us who have everything so warm and cozy just have to do something for others."

"That's what it's all about. No sense in living if we can't be helpful to those who need what we can offer. That would be sinful."

"You are absolutely right. I'll call Pastor Dan right away, and maybe when Jimmy comes tomorrow, I can tell him something that might help him.

"Good. Thanks, Iola. We were put in a place to be helpful today."

"Yes, I agree. I'll talk with you later tomorrow."

"Okay, good-bye."

21

The Young Marrieds

Now, in West Hope Church there was a group of relatively new married couples who had recently organized a class to meet on Sunday mornings during the Sunday school hour and once a month at dinner time in prearranged homes. They had enjoyed the company of one another and looked for projects that they might enjoy as outreach as well. The book of James in the New Testament was currently being studied, and Pastor Dan had recently described the small book to the class as "It is not enough to talk the Christian faith. We must live it." He had quoted James 1:22 as perhaps a good theme for their new class. "Do not merely listen to the word, and so deceive yourselves. Do what it says."

One member said, "I'm sure we can find many ways to be of help to those who need it. How can we learn of needs of those who are not even coming to church or are not part of any of our lives?"

"God will provide. Keep your eyes and ears open."

Pastor Dan directed his thinking to those energized young couples and set some action into motion that would benefit the

Adams children. There would be baskets of food, second-hand clothing, and loving and caring as the children felt inclined to receive.

The class was gaining ground in Bible study, fellowship, and now, reaching out to others. It was a worthy class and growing in many ways.

Pastor Dan knocked on Iola's door at 1:45 p.m. the next day after hearing her plea for help for the children. When he told her how eager the members of the class were, Iola was greatly relieved. She would have done the same in her day. Thankfully, the world is not all going in a backward and strange direction.

Dan told her he had called the hospital chaplain and federal privacy policies forbade him from disclosing anything personal about a patient there. The pastor would do his best to find the answers everyone was asking about Mrs. Adams. In the meantime, the children will have what they need. He also contacted the Child Welfare League of America without sharing any information with the person answering the telephone to be sure that all these fine, caring people were not doing something that might lead to the children being taken from the home.

The CWLA representative understood that the pastor had great concern for some children, and that was all that she knew.

She said, "Our focus is children and youth who may have experienced abuse, neglect, family disruption, or a range of other factors that jeopardize their safety, permanence, or well-being. CWLA also focuses on the families, caregivers, and the communities that care for and support these children. Please know that our concern for children is the same as yours. If we can ever be of service to your mission to help, give us a call. I am not going to call the officers of the court system here and encourage anything such as some kind of investigation."

"That's fine. We do hope that we can do the right things for the children; however, if we feel that we cannot, I will be in touch with you once again. Thank you very much."

He explained everything to Iola and told her he was so happy that she and Julia had notified him about what was happening right in the neighborhood. He assured her that they would not turn their backs on the children, but would care for their immediate needs and try to be in touch with their mother as soon as they could.

Iola was obviously relieved.

Jimmy arrived at her house at 2:00 p.m. as was planned. He saw Pastor Dan there and seemed pleased to see him.

Pastor Dan said a few kind words to him and asked him how his mother is doing. That opened up the door for Jimmy to tell the entire story to one who obviously was concerned for him and his family.

Pastor Dan asked Jimmy if it would be okay for some people he knew who were really nice people to carry some food and perhaps other supplies up the hill to his house.

Jimmy seemed a little uncomfortable about that but was obviously in no position to refuse those necessities of life.

"That's sure nice of them. I guess it would be okay. Would you be comin' too?"

"I would if you would want me to."

"Maybe that would be okay."

"Well, then. How about stopping by my office tomorrow afternoon, and we can work out some kind of schedule for delivery? You can be in charge of that."

Pastor Dan knew just how to make anyone feel good about anything.

"Okay, I'll do that. I'll see you at the church office tomorrow. I don't go to church, you know."

"I didn't know for sure."

"Nope, never did. But I know a lot of people who go to West Hope Church, so I guess it's okay for me to just kinda show up at the office there since you asked me to."

"Of course. That'll be fine."

After Pastor Dan left, Iola gave Jimmy a really nice knit cap to wear and sent a knitted hat and mittens to his sister. She told Jimmy that she thought they got caught up really well yesterday but as soon as more snow comes, she would like for him to work for her again.

He was smiling and seemed almost happy when he left her house.

She thanked the Lord for good, caring people and for Him leading her to call Pastor Dan.

Now she could relax. *I'll call Julia and let her know how fine this is working out. We should always try to notice the needs of others and do what we can.*

22

Two-Rific

Janine and John couldn't get enough of the babies. Every time Robert left for work, Janine volunteered to go over to the house and lend a hand, and of course, John went also. Deborah was fantastic as a new mother. Some women just naturally fall into the process, and she was one of those. She was woman and seemingly could do it all, so she really did not need much from Janine, and that was good, and Janine didn't want to be too intrusive, so she made that clear from the first.

"Look, honey, anytime I overstep my bounds or come around too much, you just say so, okay?"

"Mom, I'm sure that will never happen, but I will speak up, you know me."

Janine smiled. Yes, Deborah was always one to say it like it is, so she felt comfortable with that.

Taking care of twins was a full-time job, but Deborah somehow found the time to keep things clean including the house and the laundry. Robert was also a big help, bringing home easy-to-serve foods. Deborah had not mastered the "cooking thing" but all in good time. When Robert came home, he heated up the oven or tossed things in the microwave, sometimes put some salad supplies in a bowl, etc., and they were happy with that. The food was well-balanced and they managed well. Then after the meal, Robert would spend as much time as possible with Annette and Annabelle.

The twins were so alike at first that even the parents had trouble identifying one from the other. As time went on, Annette seemed to sleep longer than Annabelle, and she also ate more, so she gradually gained a bit more weight. That was the only way they could be sure. Then Robert wisely bought little bracelets for the girls with separate markings on them. No other person ever could figure out one from the other for a long, long time.

They were so adorable that if it had been summer, they could have taken them for strolls, and everyone would have enjoyed seeing them. But as it was still cold outdoors, they went nowhere except for doctor visits, and those were intensely demanding.

There were two of everything except the stroller, and without that, it would have been an interesting challenge.

Dr. Deloria had recommended Dr. Evelyn Nickerson as a fine pediatrician. She was present from the moment of birth for the twins, and they were on a good path to growth and good health.

The family was thrilled that the babies were here, including young Meghan and Karen. They visited Aunt Deborah often and were learning how to take care of babies. It was an interesting experience for them, and they soon adapted Annette to Meghan and Annabelle to Karen. Of course, the teens were happy with either, it just seemed to usually work out that way.

Deborah was very happy to have the girls stop over, and she tried to let them do things to help. After all, the day would come when they could babysit, and they needed to learn all about handling them as well as they possibly could.

Finally, one afternoon, it was arranged for Prince to meet the babies. Everyone was very excited to take him to Deborah's. First of all, he loved Deborah, and that was that. How would he feel now that there were babies in her house?

No one feared any trouble, only excitement. He sensed that and wondered what was going on.

"Come on, Prince, we are going to go see Deborah."

He jumped up and ran to Karen when she said it and thought, *I'm going to go see Deborah. I'm going to go see Deborah.*

He ran around the house in circles, waiting for everyone to pack into the Suburban to go.

He climbed into the car, panting, panting. The rest were smiling in anticipation.

Deborah met them at the door. Prince was permitted to go first, and when he reached her, he was so happy, but he wondered what was different today. Deborah was hugging him as usual, but she seemed different somehow. *And she smells different—a nice sweet smell.* He was happy nonetheless.

They all went together to the nursery.

The babies were awake in their individual cribs. Deborah directed Prince to Annette's bed, and he sniffed and sniffed and walked around to the other side. *What's here? It smells like Deborah.* He looked at Deborah and went nearer to almost touch the baby with his wet nose.

Deb picked up the baby and sat down on the rocking chair. "Come, Prince, see the baby."

What is that? Is it for me? He bounded over to it, and Deb said, "Easy, Prince."

He slowed down and inched his way to little Annette. Everyone else was watching and enjoying the scene. Greg had a video camera running. Prince was so good about it all. He nosed the baby and looked at Deborah again and again.

"This is Annette. It's okay. She's part of the family now."

Prince licked her little hand.

So life went on with Deborah and her little family, the Langs and their family—including Prince, of course—and John and Janine could go on with their retirement, so to speak.

Harry and his family had plans to come to Pennsylvania during Easter break, and everyone looked forward to that.

23

On the Horizon

As winter weakened, the ladies became more interested in getting back to the band and practicing for the upcoming season. They did not yet know that New York City was rising on the eastern horizon.

Yes, Janine had met with Ruth, Pastor Dan, Mr. Harris, and John too. She would go nowhere concerning this venture without John.

Mr. Harris was able to show them some videos of the show *Miracles Happen*, and Janine could certainly see her band in one such as these. She also realized that along with visiting and entertaining the folks in the nursing homes, in the senior facilities, in churches, etc., they would demonstrate to many people across the country the possibility of carrying the message of hope to others at any age. Janine came to the conclusion that it would be a very good thing for them and mostly for the television viewers to consider as something they might be able to do as well.

Mr. Harris would also come and meet with the ladies in April and discuss with them about the trip, about getting to see more of NYC, and about the show itself. So it was decided to offer the opportunity to the others. Janine would be doing that soon.

Completely unaware of any such trip possibility, Marcia Severight felt the need to offer herself to the Kitchen Band for a while to help fill the sad gap left by Adele. She had talked it over with Marvin, her husband.

"Marvin, would I be able to get away, do you think, on days when the band would be performing?"

"Why, sure! You know that our family is now helping out a lot, and you can do whatever you want to do. I've been thinking that there must be something you'd like to do away from the orchard and restaurant. You always did enjoy the work you've done at the county fair and with the local women's group, but you sure don't spend a lot of time away otherwise. I think it's great of you to suggest it, and I know you'd enjoy it. Check it out."

"Well, I think I'll speak with Janine about it. Also, being a nurse, I might just be of some help in that regard at a time or other, who knows?"

"Right! Well, let us know. We can schedule ourselves just fine."

ᴪᴪᴪ

"Janine, could I stop by some afternoon and talk with you about something?" Marcia asked.

"Of course. You could come by today if you want to."

"Oh. Well, okay. That would be super. Around one thirty?"

"I'll be here. Come on by."

That's unusual. I wonder what's on her mind?

So as one thirty came by, Janine had put on the teapot as she had learned that Marcia enjoyed tea. *A cup of hot tea would be perfect for today, and I have all these wonderful special teabags that someone gave us at Christmas.*

"Hello, Marcia. Come in, come in. This is very nice. I'm happy you could come by."

"Hi, Janine," she said as she removed her gloves, unwrapped her scarf, and pulled her boots off.

Janine, assisting her, gathered them up to a covered table left in the entry for such purposes. *The snowy weather does have some hindrances.*

"Here, let me help you with your coat. I'm beginning to have enough of the snow myself. But I do enjoy the change of seasons. I guess I'm about ready for the next change," Janine said.

Marcia laughed and said, "I prefer apple-blossom time. We live for that. The older we get the slower they come, it seems."

Finally, after all the unwrapping of outerwear, they walked together further into the house, through the living room.

"I've never seen your home here. It is beautiful. And a baby grand piano! Reminds me of my home as a child. My mother loved to play the piano, and she had a baby grand also. My brother played better than the rest of us, so he has the piano now."

"I didn't know you played," said Janine. She was delighted to learn of that.

"Well, I don't, really. I wasn't interested enough in it to practice. I was more of a tomboy than my brother was." She laughed. "I wish I had done better, but my life has been filled with other things, and that's fine."

"Sure. Well, come in the kitchen, and we'll have a cup of tea if you'd like."

"Perfect!"

They sat comfortably talking about this and that, and Janine kept wondering when she was going to get to the point of her visit. It was good to learn a little about Marcia's family, and Janine had a few questions about running an apple orchard that Marcia was happy to answer for her. Janine had always been interested in the orchard and, of course, loved the apples.

"I'm so sorry about Adele's death, Janine. She was one of the nicest women I ever knew, very quiet and very faithful. I thought of her as spiritual and devoted to caring about others. We miss her at church, and I know that the band will definitely feel the loss as well."

"Oh, we certainly will. You know, every time we gathered together privately for a lunch or dinner, she would ask the blessing, and I cherished her every word. You are right. She was spiritual and caring. The band has not been back to practice since she left. Not because of that, but because of the weather. We are going to get together again next week, I think, to practice and refigure our routine. I suppose I need to recognize that working with the elderly can lead to losses. I sure don't like that part of it."

"I know what you mean."

Silence. They each were thinking of loosing in their own private ways for a few moments.

"Well, I guess I can say what I came to say."

Janine was sure there was *something*, but what?

"I want to ask you if you think I could fill in the gap that Adele has left and use instruments such as she was using." Quickly, before there was any sort of a misunderstanding, Marcia said, "Now, please know that I would not expect to take her place. No one could do that. She was a lovely and unique woman, and I realize that I could never replace her. I'm simply thinking that I could help a little for a short while until the band kind of adjusts to her absence."

"Marcia! How wonderful of you! I'm very surprised, actually."

"Well, I'm no entertainer. I'm a little younger than the others, I suppose, and maybe they'd like to stay with the present age and lifestyle. I don't know."

"Well, I don't think that would matter at all. But my guess would be that they would like for you to come along with us. Should I ask them or what?"

"I think you should."

"Okay, I will. Thank you for offering to do that. I never expected it."

"Well, I don't know why I did. Really! It just came to me one day, and I thought, 'Okay, maybe I can do that.'"

Janine just smiled. She was astounded. Then she thought, *Why am I surprised? I should be getting used to these things. If this is God's choice, then so be it.*

Marcia asked Janine what instruments Adele had used for sure. She remembered from the church picnic that she had a violin, and she was absolutely beautiful while she played it.

"Yes, she did. She just brought that in on her own. No one even thought of a string instrument until then."

"Well, I noticed because I actually played the violin for a time. I was never really good at it, but I liked it. If it all works out, I'd like to come up with a violin."

"Yes, we will miss that in our routine unless someone takes an interest in it. So we'll see."

Janine was beginning to be excited about Marcia being in the band, but she did not want to say too much until she spoke with members of the band.

After Marcia left, Janine had to take some time to think through what just happened. Who would have dreamed that Marcia would have thought of joining the band? She was younger than the ladies, but so was Janine, and she reckoned that she and Marcia were probably the same age. Also, her age would be a benefit. She could assist others when necessary, and didn't she hear that Marcia was a nurse? Who wouldn't be glad to have a nurse on hand, especially with this group?

Hey, this is adding up to all positives. I guess I'd better make some phone calls.

24

Calling All Members . . .

"Hello!"

"Hello, Bea. This is Janine. Are you ready to get back to practicing with the band?"

"I'm wanting to, but my heart is still breaking over Adele. I don't know how I'm gonna do it without her."

"I know, I know. Me too. She was one of a kind, so lovely."

"She sure was."

"Well, we need to try, you know."

"Oh, I know. I'll be there."

"I want to ask you something. And since you were the best friend of Adele, I felt I should start with you."

"Okay."

"Marcia Severight has offered to step in to play in the band for a short time while we get adjusted to being without Adele and figure out what we need to do. Would you be comfortable with that?"

"Well, you know very well that no one can take Adele's place."

"I do. And so does Marcia. She said she could never take her place but would be glad to fill in until we get situated again."

"I think that is great of her. How could she have come up with that?"

"Who knows?"

"It would be nice to have her, I say."

"I'm glad you see it that way. I would not want to do this if it offended you or made you feel bad, Bea. I know how much you love Adele."

"Well, I don't feel bad. I feel glad."

"That's great, Bea, just great. I'll go ahead and call the others and get a consensus of opinion, and we'll see how that goes. It's good to talk with you. You take care of yourself, Bea. I would be so unhappy if anything got you down. You are so very valuable to the workings of our band, and we love you."

"No one could have said a word that would make me feel any better than what you just said. Thanks, Janine. I'll be at practice with bells on."

"Good, and thanks, Bea."

"Yep, you're welcome."

Bea felt so much better after the phone call. She had gotten so despondent over Adele's death and couldn't get to church to see anyone, and with no band practice or entertainments, she just felt like curling up in a tiny ball and letting the world go by.

But hey! Come on, girl. You've got a band to play in. You're having practice next week, and you had better brighten up and get going. No one wants to see a sluggish bee. That's not me. No sirree! Ha-ha! That's a rhyme! She stood up, straightened herself to her full height of probably less than five feet, and said out loud, "That's not me. No sirree!"

ˠˠˠ

"Hello!"

"Hello, Anne. This is Janine. How are you?"

"Oh, fair enough, I guess."

"And Owen?"

"He's had his share of colds and such, but he's doing well right now."

"Oh dear. We all need some warm weather, don't you think?"

"Yes, that would be nice."

"We have band practice next week. Are you planning to get out for that?"

"If the weather is okay, yes. Would you mind if Owen came with me?"

"No, I would not mind. I'd be happy to have him come. He's one of our encouragers. Bring him along. That's fine.

"Something interesting has happened. Marcia Severight has volunteered to fill in for awhile until we can adjust to Adele being gone. How would you feel about that?"

"Fine, just fine. Marcia is enjoyable to have around. What got into her to have her want to do this?"

"I don't know. She seems to feel drawn to do it, and I think it would be nice to have her. But I want the members of the band to decide if they feel okay about it all."

"Well, I feel fine about that. I say we can use help any time."

"Well, good. Thanks. Have you been feeling well during these bleak days?"

"I feel a lot better now that the sun is trying to come out."

"Me too. Well, we'll see you on Tuesday."

"Okay, thanks for calling."

Owen was resting, so she didn't tell him about the practice just yet. She would later. He would enjoy going along. She also thought about Marcia and her offer. *That's really nice of her. I think she'll enjoy herself, and we'll enjoy her.*

ϒϒϒ

"Hello, Julia. This is Janine."

"Hello, Janine. It's good to hear from you. How are you?"

"Good. Deborah had her baby girl twins. They are identical twins and beautiful."

"Oh, yes, the word spread around here pretty fast. Congratulations! How special. I had twins but one died. I hope your twins are both strong and healthy."

"Yes, they are, thanks. How have you been? I haven't seen you in a few weeks."

"Believe it or not, I have been perfectly well all winter," Julia said.

"That's wonderful! I'm so glad. I've been too busy to even notice if I'm well or not."

"I can imagine. Well, you have so much to look forward to now. Do you think you'll have time to keep on working with the band?"

"Are you kidding? I love the band. It's one of my very favorite things. I can't wait for us to get going again."

Julia was relieved of her thoughts. It crossed her mind every once in a while that the band may not continue.

"Oh, that's good. I was afraid that you might want to spend a lot of time with the babies and might not be able to do so with the responsibilities of the band."

"Well, the band is very high on my priority list, believe me. We have practice next week. I'll pick you up at the usual time. But I have something I want to ask you. It's about Marcia Severight."

"Marcia. What do you want to know?"

"Well, she has offered to join up with the band for a while until we figure what to do with Adele's instrumental parts in the scheme of things. How would you feel about that?"

"Well, she's younger than we are, but I would like having her with us."

"She's about my age, I think."

"I'd guess you are right."

"So you are okay with her coming along and being in the band right now?"

"Yes, I am. I'm glad she wants to be with us. I'm sorry about Adele, though. She was such a beautiful and sincere lady."

"I agree. We will miss her so much."

"I suppose we might as well face up to the fact that we will be losing our band as time goes on."

"Not for a long time, I hope!"

"Me too."

When Julia hung up, she was smiling because she was relieved to know that the band was going to play on. So much of her happiness during the past year or so had been attributed to her activities within the band, and she knew that keeping up with that will mean a lot to her future. She had finally felt acceptance and believed she was actually one with all the rest.

ϒϒϒ

Iola paused in the kitchen and wondered if she heard her telephone ringing or not. She looked across the room, and the light on the receiver was flashing, indicating that a call was coming in. "Oh dear! The phone is ringing. I wonder if I can get to it in time."

She scurried across the floor and answered it. "Hello, hello!"

Nothing.

"Well, I guess I was too late. Let me see who it was. Oh, it was Janine. Maybe I can call her back and catch her."

"Hello!"

"Janine, this is Iola. I think you tried to call me, but I didn't hear the phone soon enough."

"Oh, yes, Iola. That's fine. Thanks for calling me back. How have you been?"

"Oh, not too bad. I just wish Old Man Winter would go back where he came from. He makes me miserable and shivery and also lonely. I haven't seen many people for months. I think the funeral was the last time I really went anywhere."

"Yes. Maybe we all need to move to the South. Those people surely do have it better this time of year. But I don't think I could take the summers in the humidity and heat, do you?"

"No, not really."

"Iola, I had a visit from Marcia Severight the other day, and she volunteered to jump into the band and participate in Adele's place for a short time while we figure out what to do. We decided that I would talk it over with the band members and see what you all thought. Now you don't have to say it's fine if you feel any apprehension about this. Just think it over and tell me exactly what you think, okay?"

"Well, I would not have a problem with Marcia being a participant in the band at all. How nice of her to even consider doing that for us. She could play the violin and whatever else Adele used to do and it certainly would be helpful for now. We are going to miss Adele so much, Janine. She has been a dear friend to all of us and very special."

"I know that, Iola. I too will miss her. But I agree that Marcia was good to suggest helping us out. I never ever would have thought she would be interested."

"She is usually so busy with the orchard and the restaurant there."

"She told me that her family is slowly taking on the responsibilities of the apples, and others are practically running the restaurant these days. She can get away when she wants to, and she thinks she would truly enjoy the mission work of the band."

"That's it, then. I vote yes."

"That's good. Will you be at practice next week?'

"Yes. I'm looking forward to it very much."

What Iola didn't say was that she was counting the days. The winter made her feel old, and she didn't like that at all. She always felt better in the summer when she could be out and more active.

♈♈♈

"Hello, Rachael. This is Janine. How are you?"

"Hello, Janine. I was just thinking about you. How are the twins?"

"You cannot believe how beautiful they are, and there are two of them."

"I know. How wonderful. Congratulations to you and the family. I suppose we'll get to see them in the summer. I hope so, anyway."

"I hope so too."

"How are you getting around these days?" Janine asked.

"Well, the cold is too cold, the snow is too slippery, and my arthritis is not cooperating very well, but I am feeling much better in general. I'm ready to get back into the swing of things especially with the band."

"I am too. Let me brush something by you. Marcia Severight visited me and volunteered to participate in our band for a time while we transition through the loss of Adele. What do you think?"

"I can't believe it. How wonderful of her. Are you saying she would be a member even though she isn't one of the old ladies?"

"Look, you aren't so old, and she is no spring chicken. She's my age at least. Why not? It's all part of the mission of love regardless of real age, don't you think?"

"Yes, I do. I'm just so impressed that she would enter into this knowing that the rest of us are considerably over the hill. But if she thinks she would enjoy it, that's great. I say let her in."

"I thought you'd say that."

"I can't wait to get back to the band. I did worry some about what we would do concerning the parts that Adele had. I guess the good Lord answered our prayers and sent us Marcia."

"You know, I feel that too. He must want us to keep on playing, so we will, right?"

"Right. Will you be stopping by for me for practice?"

"Of course. I'll see you then."

Rachael was so happy to be finally getting on with life. She had been recuperating for a couple of years from a very bad accident. Now she was ready to do more and looked forward to the season of entertaining once again. The time was really right for her. She had other irons in the fire also with some fantastic crafts she was working up, so she had kept busy through the wintertime on those.

ϒϒϒ

Janine had difficulty reaching Pauline, so she finally left a message for her to return the call.

"Hello."

"Hello, Janine. I'm sorry to miss your calls. I was out of town, but don't worry, I remembered the practice and can't wait to be there. My trombone has been fidgeting to get going again."

"Good, that's fine. I want to ask you a question though. Marcia Severight offered to participate in the band with us until we figure out what to do about Adele's part. How would you feel about that?"

"My goodness. I feel good about that. No one can ever replace Adele, of course, but to have a joyful personality such as Marcia care enough to help us through this is utterly fantastic. I would have no problem with that at all."

"I think it's a great idea too. How have you been?"

"Well, no real problems at this time, thankfully. I've spent a bit of time on my paintings and then left to visit relatives in the Midwest. That was a nice break, but I'm ready to get rolling with the band. I miss it so much."

"I know what you mean. We'll have a lot to do this year."

Janine didn't tell anyone about the New York invitation yet. She wanted to have them all together and let them discuss it together.

"Well, we'll see you next week."

"Great. I can't wait."

So all calls were made. They were all lifted by the conversations and by Marcia's consideration for them and her desire to help.

25

The More We Get Together, the Happier We'll Be

Janine zipped out the road to pick up Rachael, hardly noticing that it had not warmed up as she had expected, but she knew that they had to get together now because they had engagements coming up in another week or so, and there was much to be done. She also wanted to inform them about the New York City proposition next week. She planned to give it another week before bringing it up.

She tooted the horn and drove by the house to turn around. When she made the turn, there stood Rachael with her bag of instruments, but the smile she carried was much more important than anything in that bag.

Janine stopped the car, got out, and hurried to the steps to lend a hand.

"Hello, hello," she said. "Where is your cane?"

"Well, I've been walking all winter to get myself away from that cane, and last week, the doctor commended me and said I don't really need it. My balance is good and so is my confidence."

"Isn't that wonderful? But please be careful on the steps. They could still be a little icy," Janine said.

"Oh, I'm sure they are fine. Albert came over this morning and saw to that. He does not want me to fall so he keeps everything salted down or shoveled clear."

"Here. Can I at least carry your bag?"

"That would be just fine. Thanks so much."

They both handled the situation perfectly and were in the car, driving to pick up Julia in the town.

Janine got out of the car and saw that her steps were definitely clear. She knocked on the door, which Julia opened immediately.

One good thing was that Julia was very sure on her feet and did not need a cane or walker and never did. Also, there is a very solid iron railing all the way down. Julia was ready with her coat and gloves on, and Janine picked up her very light bag. Her instruments thus far were small, so this was fairly easy.

She closed up the house, led Julia down, and they both did just fine. Julia took Janine's arm, and she was in the car without any problems at all.

Julia and Rachael were happy to see each other and to be starting up practice again.

When they arrived at the church, which was just a short turn from Julia's house, they drove up the hill and noticed that the others had already arrived.

Behind Janine was Marcia, so they all got out of their cars and with Janine and Marcia's assistance walked over to the beautiful red front doors.

The church was warm as the minister had been in for a few hours and knew they were coming. He was glad to turn the thermostat higher to accommodate them.

"Mmm, it feels nice and warm in here."

Pastor Dan peeked out of his office and welcomed them with a big smile and hugs.

They were meeting in the sanctuary today, so they all removed their heavy coats and hung them up and took everything down to the front of the pews. They knew that, as usual, Janine would have something to say to them first.

"Ladies, it is so good to see all of you here. We have a lot to do and preparations to make, and we could not have waited any longer. I'm receiving invitations now and then, and they are piling up. I want to go over what I have with you before we get into practicing today.

"But before we can begin, we all want to give a big, hearty welcome to dear Marcia for joining with us today. Marcia, welcome."

Everyone clapped their hands and said words of welcome aloud to Marcia. She stood long enough to say thanks and said she was happy to be with them. She also said, "I don't know if I can keep up with you all, but we'll see."

Everyone was in a good mood, and Janine got out her schedule and ran through the list of appointments they needed to confirm. There was a one-hundredth birthday party for a man who was acquainted with the folks at West Hope but not a member. They agreed to go and said, "We'll have to sing 'Happy Birthday' to him."

Three were from senior centers in the region, two churches invited them to come for lunch and entertain, a women's group from another denomination invited them to dinner and entertainment, and there was one from a community that Janine knew nothing about.

"Where is this?" she asked.

"Isn't that the new independent church built out over the hills on Route 16?" asked Pauline.

"Yes, the caller said it is a new church."

"That's what I thought."

"How far?" Janine asked.

"Well, maybe twenty miles or so."

"Should we do that?"

"I think it would be fine. You said that we would have dinner catered by Edward's didn't you?" Bea joined in.

"Yes, that's what the caller said."

"Hey, that would be so delicious, and it would give us an opportunity to reach out a bit to a new place. I think we should go," Bea answered, and everyone agreed.

"Okay with me," said Janine.

"In May, we have a request for every week, and one week in May, two, because a lot of folks think we would be perfect for mother-daughter dinners. I'm not sure that we can do all these. Maybe we can sort them out a bit."

"No, no, that's fine" was the unanimous opinion.

"And guess what? We've been invited back to Serenity House."

Everyone gladly responded affirmatively to that.

"Okay, the birthday party is the first week of June. Let's not get too far booked ahead right now." She was thinking of the New York City trip, but they agreed to comply, and then moved on with practice.

"I just want to say to all of you that I realize that we have an adjustment to make due to our devastating loss of our beloved Adele. I truly believe she would not want us to drop our mission work but to honor her by continuing. I am very sure that the Lord has nudged dear Marcia to help us do that. Knowing that Adele is rejoicing in heaven, let us rejoice here in her memory until we are called to join her with the band of angels."

No one really spoke, but all nodded in agreement. Finally, Bea jumped up and picked up her bag and said, "Let's get on with this."

Janine lined them up and placed Marcia in Adele's place. Marcia did not have any instruments with her, but Bea was prepared. No one would have expected what happened next.

Bea picked up another bag, and she sat down on the first pew facing the lineup of musicians and pulled from the bag Adele's instruments.

They were all stunned and didn't know how to react.

Bea said, "When Billie brought these to me, I was absolutely sure that I would never use them and I would never bring them here for anyone else to use. They've been in my living room for the past few weeks.

"Last night, I decided to look at them. After a little while, I felt without a doubt that Adele would rather have someone continue the use of them than to have them just sit around and do no good whatsoever. So I think that Marcia should use them. What do you all think?"

Everyone was fine about it, and Marcia said she would be happy to give it a try.

"Marcia, I have new kazoos. Maybe you'd like your own to attach onto the horn."

"Okay, thank you. The violin she made from a wall-plaque wooden spoon is so beautiful. I'll try that too. And what are these?"

"They are maracas. We used them in the Mexican song and dance," said Pauline.

"Oh yes. Is there a hat?"

"I have the hats," Janine said, "but you could come up with a hat to use for the entry parade, I think. Anything will do. Make it funny."

"Okay, I'll try."

"Yes, and we have country straw hats now. Was Adele's in the bag?" asked Rachael.

"No, no hats," Bea said.

"What do I need?"

"Straw, most likely. You'll see the others today, and you can design one for yourself, if that's okay with you," Janine said.

"Sure, that's fine. I don't know how to use a kazoo."

"Well, don't worry. Iola is a great teacher," said Janine. "I'm going to excuse myself for a few minutes. Iola, will you help her put the kazoo on the horn here, and we'll get started as soon as I return."

With that, Janine left the room to go to the restroom. She really didn't need to but thought the time spent with busy hands and conversations was needed to break the tension a bit, and she was fairly exhausted with stressfulness about wanting everything to go well today. She didn't have a thing to worry about as it turned out. These ladies could handle anything!

Marcia was nervous. She was happy to be there but wondered if she would fit in and if they would wish she hadn't come to fill in. As time went on, and after flubbing up the kazoo a few times, she was getting the hang of it all. She thought she'd learn, and everyone encouraged her to not worry.

"Don't even think about it. We never do the same things all the time. Sometimes we don't even know what we're doing. It doesn't matter. We're supposed to be funny, and we usually are—right or wrong," Bea said.

"Okay."

At the end of practice, Janine reminded them all that they had one more practice before the first outing, so she strongly encouraged everyone to be there next week. Of course, she knew that she had to bring up the New York project next week as well.

Everyone would be there. Marcia said that she had asked Jackie to clear out the little room for them to have lunch.

Owen had attended the practice with Anne. They both decided it best to go on home. Owen said he had a fine time today and thought the band was really good. That made everyone feel even happier.

The rest of them were going to the restaurant together as usual, so they cleaned up, told Pastor Dan they were leaving, and got into their respective cars.

What a day! Janine was counting her blessings as she drove home. She had more than usual this year for sure.

Marcia ate with them rather than go to the kitchen, and she fit right in.

All was well.

26

Guess What?

The second practice went very well. Marcia could actually play the kazoo, and she sure didn't mind giving all she could to dancing with the maracas and sombrero. She knew how to hold the bow and take it beautifully across the strings of the violin. She still had work to do on a couple of hats, but she would have them for the performance in a few days.

They went entirely through the routine twice, much to Owen's delight. He truly enjoyed himself at the practices, and might even go along to the next performance with his wife. They were going to a senior center, and he would certainly be welcome there.

They arranged time and transportation and were finished with all they needed to do to be ready.

"Ladies, I need to speak to you for a minute. Something has come up that surprised me, and it will no doubt surprise you as well. Take a seat, please."

"I received a telephone call from a Mr. Harris a few weeks ago. He is employed by FBN."

"FBN? Faith Broadcasting Network?" asked Rachael.

"Yes."

"Faith Broadcasting Network? Why?" Bea asked.

"Well, Mr. Harris had read about our performance for the ministers at Christmas that was written up in the *Pittsburgh Sunday Paper* in December. He said the Associated Press had picked it up. You know, I thought something might come of that article. I said at the time that this could be the beginning of something for us to do in the Pittsburgh area. And we have had a couple of calls from that direction, but Mr. Harris was calling from New York.

"He said he was very interested in the mission of The Band of Hope and wants to do a story for the television station about us."

"My goodness!" said Julia.

"I know. I think that would be really wonderful, don't you?"

"Well, I never dreamed . . ." responded Anne.

"What did he want you to do?" asked Iola.

"Well, he wants to talk with all of you about going to New York to tape a show."

Well, the response from those ladies could be described as explosive. Everyone began to talk at once. Questions were being asked one over the other. Janine had to quiet them down to say anything more.

"Look, I know this is shocking. I felt the same way when he talked with me, but the longer we go along, the more I realize that this is a good thing. We have an opportunity to spread the joy of the Lord in a new way and on national TV, and others can catch on and maybe try to follow in these steps and have the same success as we have had. It's really a great opportunity."

"I have no idea how on earth we can do this," Iola said. "What's he expect of us? Do we go by train, plane, bus, or what?"

"He said the broadcasting station would provide transportation."

"When?"

"I'm not sure. We talked about going this summer. Mr. Harris is coming here next week to answer all your questions. I don't have many answers myself yet."

"I've never been to New York. Are we talking about New York City?" asked Julia.

"Yes."

"My heavens!" she responded.

The others were sitting there so astounded that they almost couldn't even talk. Finally Rachael asked, "Would we do our routine for the program? What program are we talking about? I've watched FBN."

"I have too," several threw in.

"It is *Miracles Happen*," Janine said.

"They sure do," said Pauline. "It is a miracle that we are together doing what we do. I have dreamed of being in New York entertaining. I have! When I was a girl, I pretended that I was there and I was dancing. Of course, I might have had a better chance if I had taken dance lessons."

They laughed at that, but they believed Pauline. She had a natural talent for the stage. She just seemed to come alive when she entertained. She was never nervous but, rather, excited each and every time.

Anne said, "Owen and I have been to New York City, haven't we?"

"Yes. It is a wonderful, exciting place to visit. I'm very interested in this conversation. I hope you don't mind me sitting in on it."

"Not at all," Janine spoke for all of them.

"Well, thank you. I would be happy if Anne went back. And she knows I would be fine here for a few days or whatever. Our daughter would see to that. There is a lot to see in New York. Maybe you'd get a chance to look around a bit. It would be something to share along with an experience that very few can claim."

Well, good for Owen. He said it well, Janine thought.

"How do the rest of you feel?" Janine asked.

"I am too overwhelmed to even think straight, but I honestly hope it is real," Julia said. "I never ever would have thought to go to New York City. I'd love to see the Statue of Liberty."

"Well, you may have a chance to do that," said Janine.

"I'm glad I got past having to use a cane," said Rachael.

"I don't want to get too excited over this yet," said Iola. "We need more information. If we have to pay out a lot of money, it would be close to impossible for us to go, I think."

"Mr. Harris will answer those questions next week, but he did say all expenses will be paid. I know this sounds too good to be true, so maybe it is. We'll find out for sure next week. I just wanted to prepare you ahead of meeting with him."

If anyone walked into the room at that point, they would see a group of ladies staring into space with many thoughts going through their minds. At that point, they were nearly speechless.

"May I suggest that we don't go around talking about this beyond our own families? Like Iola says, we need more information before we can say for sure how we will answer this request."

"Right, I agree," said Iola.

Marcia broke in, "Ladies, if we are finished, Jackie has made a fresh pot of green pepper soup and is expecting us about now. What do you say, Janine?"

"That's great. Let's go."

The ladies were buzzing with excitement but were very careful not to speak out so that the diners wouldn't hear them. They all received a cup of soup on the house, and a few ordered a dessert to follow.

"Marcia, how do you feel about the trip? You haven't said anything," asked Janine.

"Oh, that's because I shouldn't be sticking my nose in. I'm not really a tried-and-true member like the rest of you and would not be expecting to go on the trip."

Everyone told her not to say that. They wanted her to feel included and to begin to think about it with them as well.

Janine was thinking that having a nurse along would be an exceptionally good thing. *It's incredibly interesting how things work out.*

27

Marcia's Debut

The ladies were very excited to be back in the entertainment business as they loaded up in cars and headed out to the MacLintock Senior Center in a neighboring county. The sunshine warmed them inside and out, and they chattered about many things on the hour-long trip.

No one had been to the facility before, so they were all curious as to what they would find.

Marcia drove her daughter's van and had all the equipment, in addition to three of the band members. Janine, as usual, had Julia, Rachael, and Iola with her. Iola had thought she would drive herself and stop at Macy's at the mall on the way home, but decided that she'd prefer to do that another day.

The beautiful driveway led to an entrance that was breathtakingly beautiful. It was a large mansion in the Queen Anne style with turrets and irregular but lovely roof shapes.

A very nice young woman met them at the door and offered her assistance to help carry any of the musical instruments, which was indeed helpful. They unloaded everything in a short time and were directed to a lovely dining room set with tulips, daffodils, and pastel tablecloths.

"We'll just put your instruments over here. Please come and sit at these tables reserved for you. We are so thrilled to have you come today. Lunch will be served in about ten minutes, and then we would like for you to go right ahead and start your program for us, if that's all right with you."

Janine replied, "Yes, of course. This facility is so very nice. You have a beautiful senior center here. I'm wondering if it was a family residence or if it was built for some other purpose?"

"It was actually a gambling hall and speakeasy back in earlier times. We've heard some fascinating stories about what actually went on here. But that was in the distant past, and we have found this to be a fine place to meet for lunch and events planned throughout the year."

"Well, how interesting. I love the wraparound porch and the turrets and gables. It all seems so proper and lovely that it's hard to imagine that it was built for gambling purposes."

"We love it! It is so perfect for our seniors. We all feel as though we are reliving an earlier time in history when we come here. You'll notice that we have a big turnout today. They are very excited to have The Band of Hope come all the way here to entertain. When we read of your mission in the newspaper, we were all hoping you could come."

"Thank you, we're happy to be here."

"Oh, I see lunch is ready."

They ate a lovely light lunch of little sandwiches, fresh fruits, cottage cheese, and crackers, and sherbet for dessert.

Marcia was getting nervous and anxious to finish and get on with the program. She felt excitement as well and hoped she could fit in.

She did! She was wonderful, and her joy in the project radiated from her. The band members caught on to her excitement, and each and every one of them was even a tad bit better that day than always before. The audience sang along, laughed throughout, and stood for a hand-clapping finale.

As usual, the band enjoyed the high jinks and craziness as much as the audience. Their style of spreading the joy of the Christian life was accepted and appreciated by everyone there, and The Band of Hope lifted the spirits and gave everyone something to think about as well.

As they were getting into their cars, Janine asked Marcia what she thought about being in the band that day.

"Janine, I haven't had so much fun in years! I felt younger and more alive than usual, and it gave me such pleasure to know that I was serving the Lord's purpose even in a pretty far-fetched manner. Who would have ever thought it?"

"No one could have dreamed this act up, Marcia. It was brought to us by the Holy Spirit, and He sure must love a good time because He certainly has given us a lot of it."

"Janine, I do believe I was led to be in the band, and I'm grateful beyond words."

All the band members felt the same about what they are doing. Only they could really know the value of a zany kitchen band who dreamt up silly instruments and shared laughter in the Lord's name.

They were on the road again, and they were about to do something they never dreamed of doing. They are talking about New York City between themselves as though it was inevitable, with nothing to stand in the way.

ϒϒϒ

Marcia jumped through her kitchen door with her entertainment hat on, and announced herself to Marvin with hands high overhead, "Ta-da!"

Marvin was startled by her boisterous entrance but enjoyed it nonetheless.

"Hello! You look happy. I'm assuming that things went well."

"Everything went well. It was wonderful and fun, and the audience enjoyed the entertainment too. I have watched the band before and thought they were having a good time, but I'll tell you, no one can really have any idea what fun it is."

"Well, I guess you have shown your qualifications and are officially a member of the band, right?"

"I guess so. I can't believe it. How did this happen? I hadn't thought about it ever before, but for some reason after Adele died, I couldn't get the band out of my mind. Janine and I both believe I volunteered because I was lead to do so by the Lord. That's the only answer, and I'm very happy about it.

"We are going to be busy in the next couple of months. I have the schedule. I didn't post it to the refrigerator as I thought I should wait until I made it through the first real time in front of an audience, but here it is!" She lifted a magnet and placed the schedule under it on the door.

"There are lots of places to go because the band got one terrific write-up in the Sunday paper that I showed you weeks ago. Janine says the telephone keeps ringing. We're going to get business cards. Ha! Isn't this something?"

"It sure is." Marvin walked over to the list posted on the refrigerator, and at the very end of the list was New York City.

"Marcia, what's this?"

"New York City."

"I know, but why is it here?"

"What do you think?"

"Beats me!"

She didn't answer. She took off her hat and put it in the bag she was carrying with her instruments, and let him ponder it for a few minutes.

He turned to her and raised his eyebrows and said, "Come on, now, tell me."

"It's hard to believe."

"Try me."

"There is a faith-based television broadcasting network in New York City called FBN that has learned of The Band of Hope and has invited us to go to New York and be on the program *Miracles Happen*."

"You're right, I don't think I can believe it."

"I can hardly believe it either, but I guess it's true. Mr. Harris from the network has been talking with Janine, and she says it is on the up-and-up. He is actually coming to talk with the band members next Tuesday."

"Well, well, whadayaknow!"

"We have lots of questions to ask him, so we are not sure about doing this yet. Don't say anything to anyone until we have all the information and have decided whether or not this would be something we can manage. I don't mean financially—apparently it won't cost us—but physically. The ladies are all so excited about it, and they think they can do it, so it may actually happen."

"When?"

"I think this summer."

"Well, that's great. Just great! Will you get to go too?"

"They all say I would have to go with them."

"Good, let's see what happens. I think it's terrific, Marcia. The little town of West Hope has produced something pretty special. We may find our town on the map with this and have more people stopping by to find out more about you all. Ha! How about that?"

"I don't know what to say. Just wait and see."

28

Pleasures and Fixins

In the meantime, the adventures of Annette and Annabelle were moving on. Deborah and Robert were naturally tired most of the time even though members of the family would love to take over for several hours at a time. The parents of the twins were so thrilled to have them in their lives that they could not imagine being apart from them. Robert had shortened his working hours, and that helped Deborah considerably. The girls were still identical to the world and adorable. They have very light-colored hair that tended to curl when wet, and their eyes were as blue as the sky.

Annette almost rolled over last week and startled herself. The cooing practice had begun, and nothing was so wonderful as to imagine than a baby actually trying to communicate with a parent.

Harry, Rhonda, and the three boys would be visiting soon, and the entire family—from Mom and Dad to sisters, brothers-in-law, nieces, and cousins—were looking forward to the visit. Some had not seen the boys for two years, and that was just too long!

Janine and John were very interested in each and every member of their family. The bigger it grew, the better.

No one is going to meet them at the airport because Harry has rented an SUV to be picked up at the airport. He said he would want to have the wheels during the week anyway, and his family needed a lot of car space with luggage and a lot of humanity. So next Friday, they would arrive a little past 4:00 p.m.

Janine has a great deal on her mind with expectations running high concerning Mr. Harris's visit this week, and she was planning meals and making room for each of the boys. Harry and Rhonda would have a bedroom, and the boys would sleep on sleeping bags that their father had suggested as the best accommodation for them anyway. The downstairs would hold three boys without any problem, and they would have their own bathroom there and even a kitchen equipped with a refrigerator filled with fruit, milk, and juices.

It would be wonderful! However, Janine was presently on her way to pick up her riders to go to the church to meet with Mr. Harris. She was quite nervous about it. She was feeling a huge responsibility and couldn't shake off the uneasiness she felt about the trip and the ladies remaining in good health throughout. *We can never be sure with the elderly. Their balance is not one hundred percent. Sometimes they forget to do the things they planned to do, and they might eat something that could make them sick.*

Okay! That's enough of that. I'm not in charge. First of all, I know that the Lord will see this through if it is right to do, and Mr. Harris will see to it that they are taken good care of, won't he?

29

I Have a Plan for You

Janine, Julia, and Rachael arrived at the church first. They went inside, and there was Pastor Dan ready to welcome them.

"Hello, ladies. You must be very excited about coming here today. I'm aware of the entire situation and have met Mr. Harris already. I'm excited for you. Let's wait and see if it all sounds like something you want to do. I've been invited to sit in on this session. I hope you don't mind."

Rachael said, "I think that's just as it should be. I'm glad you will be here with us, Pastor."

Pauline came through the door alone. Since she lived in a different community, she sometimes drove her car and met up with the rest.

"Hi, everyone! I'm so excited today. I sure hope this goes well."

Janine answered, "We all do, Pauline. But one never knows. Let's just try to learn all that we can so that we can make the right decisions."

"Right! That's what we should do," Pauline replied.

The others came in almost at the same time. Pastor Dan greeted them and suggested that they go on into the sanctuary, and he would stay behind to greet Mr. Harris.

The ladies were all nervously talking and saying pretty much the same things. They sure did need answers to a lot of questions, and they were about to get those answers because Mr. Harris was right on time.

He and Pastor Dan came down front and greeted the women, and Pastor Dan suggested they sit down and let Janine and Mr. Harris face them in the front to take over the meeting.

Janine introduced Mr. Harris, who was not really tall but carried himself with dignity and was sporting a slight beard that seemed to be the fashion in the larger cities of America. He was wearing a very fine camel overcoat with a plaid scarf and leather gloves, and he removed all of those. Janine very carefully laid them across one of the pews.

"Ladies, it is a pleasure to meet you. I've been looking forward to this for quite some time. We have a lot to think about, a lot to talk about, and probably a lot to pray about. I wonder if it would be all right with you if I opened this conversation with a short prayer to our Lord?"

Well, he sure made some points with that because the ladies had learned to turn to the Lord with their joys and sorrows and for answers to questions too. They were delighted to have him say that.

"Of course," Janine replied.

Each bowed her head. It was assumed that Pastor Dan did also.

"Almighty God, Creator of the world and Father of us all, we call upon you to be with us this day as we meet to make decisions. Help us to do what is right in your sight. Be our guide. Be our comforter. Touch us with your peace, and ever and always be our strength. We pray in the name of your Son, Jesus. Amen."

A general feeling of peace did fall upon them, and they were ready to hear from the man from New York City about what might be in their future.

"The Faith Broadcasting Network's mission is to lead others to Jesus Christ. We believe He is the Way, the Truth, and the Light, just as you do. There are millions of others who do not believe that, and so our mission is large because we have the means to reach out to thousands and thousands. We are now broadcasting from sea to shining sea. It has taken ten years to finally reach that goal, which is really not that long if you knew the difficulties of achieving that. I won't go into those details. It is just a good thing to know that we are eager to find stories to be broadcast that might lift the spirits of many, and we pray that with each and every story there are many who will find the encouragement to live a life for Jesus.

"Your story is one of a kind. When I read about it, *my* spirits were lifted! I am amazed to hear about your creativity, your energies, your desire for touching lives with the joy of the Lord, and that you are senior citizens to boot! This is fantastic. You have so much to offer to others. You can lift spirits, I know. You could also encourage other seniors, or maybe even those not yet in that age, to do something. Yes, do something—your message says that so clearly.

"How do you feel about what you do?"

No one expected a question here, so they didn't respond right away.

"Well, you might think it's a lot of effort on our part, but really, I love it. I love getting up in the morning and knowing we have a place to go, people to meet, and love to share," Bea said.

"And also, it's something to think about on days when I'm all alone with no one to talk with. I can try to think up something for the band to do, like a different instrument or something to add to my hat, and think about those things. Before we started this band, I was really lonesome and felt that my life was pretty much used up."

Bea said it so well, and yet others wanted to express their thoughts as well.

Rachael echoed Bea's words about being used up and said she found a real reason to keep living. She had a very bad automobile accident that everyone thought would be the end of her efforts to be creative and active. "But I love the band so much that I just had to get stronger again and get back with it. I feel really alive again and have a purpose for living."

"I know what Rachael means," said Julia. "It's hard to grow old when your husband is gone, your sisters and brothers are gone, and your children have moved away to find good employment. I used to sit in my house alone for weeks on end and maybe see no one, especially in the winter time. Now I have something to do, like you said, Mr. Harris—something to do and also bring joy to others. It's a blessing."

Pauline said she really enjoyed entertaining. She always did, but for years now, all she did to really make herself happy was paint pictures by herself. "It was something to do, of course, and I felt good doing it but had no one to share any time with or make plans together. Now I'm having the time of my life."

Mr. Harris felt their emotions concerning the band. Most everyone needed someone. He heard once that the three elements to happiness were having someone to love, having something to do, and having someone to do it with. He thought the ladies were demonstrating that pretty well. First and foremost would be belief in the Lord and His guidance, then spreading the love and joy of the Christian life as something to do, and following that with sharing their joy together as sisters in mission as the final of the three elements.

He didn't mention it at the time, but it was clearly proven out to be their happiness.

The talk went on for a while as the ladies felt free to open up their thoughts with Mr. Harris. They were all much more at ease, and it was time to talk with them about the details of the trip.

"My idea is to have you go to New York City for perhaps two and a half days. On the final day, we would have an audience for you to perform some of your routine. We'd have to time it out and decide which parts of the routine would be selected by you and the producer. Here's what we would have to do: We'd like for you to go to the studio where the broadcast would take place, put on your outfits, and just go ahead and perform like you always do. Then together we can decide what would go into the recorded performance later. That's no problem, I'm sure. Everybody okay with that?"

No one objected.

"Okay, so that won't take up a great deal of your time. You'll have time to do other things. If you arrive in the early afternoon, we can get you to a hotel and have you freshen up and maybe rest for an hour or so and then do something. I have a good idea about a bus tour that takes you around to some interesting parts of the city. It is a two-hour tour, but you can get off the bus at one or so of the sights, look around all you want to, and there will always be another of the tour buses coming by to pick you up and move on to the next spot."

"What places would we be likely to see?" asked Iola.

"Well, this one is called downtown tour hop-on, hop-off. It lists Rockefeller Center, Times Square, the Empire State Building, Greenwich Village, Little Italy, Saint Paul's Chapel, the World Trade Center site, Wall Street, Battery Park, and the United Nations building. There are others just like this. We can talk all about it later on. Another thing this brochure says is, 'All our double-decker buses use clean-air technology.'

"This would be an easy way to get around and see as much as possible. We have people who would be going along with you everywhere you go. It's an awesome city, and we want you to enjoy it without getting uncomfortable at any time."

The ladies were relieved and thinking that all sounded great.

"Another thing I know that you would enjoy would be to go to a Broadway show. Am I right?"

"Right" was the unanimous consensus.

"Well, we can have you go to a matinee. My thought is to get you to New York early on a Tuesday. We can accomplish the tour on that day, and later after dinner, go through your routine with the producer and prop people.

"Then on Wednesday morning, take your time, have a nice lunch, and go to the show of your choice. We'll have to preorder tickets, so that will be decided soon. This would be an easy day for you because we would prerecord the segment for *Miracles Happen* at around 7:00 p.m. that evening, and we wouldn't want to tire you out going from here to there all day Wednesday."

"Thursday you would be returning home. There might be an early part of the day to go sightseeing some more, but that depends upon the time of the flight back to Pittsburgh."

They were thinking, *So we are going to fly.*

So Iola just jumped in and asked, "Are we flying then?"

"Oh, I'm sorry. I forgot to talk about transportation. Yes, we've seen a good flight out of Pittsburgh that goes into Kennedy International, and from there to the hotel, you will go by company limo."

Good heavens! They were really taken aback. Everything up until this was so exciting they could hardly keep from jumping up and dancing, but when he said *limo*, everyone nearly lost it.

"Oh my goodness!" Pauline said. "I've always wanted to ride inside of a limousine."

Mr. Harris said he realized that it might seem like a special thing to do, and of course, it was truly great, but in New York City, the taxis took over and they would not want to separate the band members from one another. There was also the luggage to consider. Taxis were hectic and could be a pretty frantic way of being introduced to New York.

"We use our limo because the passengers enjoy it and because it is the most efficient way to transport a group of people through the city. I believe you will enjoy the ride.

"Well, we've gone over a lot here. Are there questions?"

Janine was sitting there, observing the ladies, and she knew he had convinced them that they should go on this adventure. She sat back and listened.

"Who is paying for all these things you have mentioned, such as airplanes, limos, hotel, meals, tours?" asked Iola.

"The network is paying for it all" was his answer.

"That's going to be a lot of money, Mr. Harris," said Marcia.

"Well, not really. We figure we are getting our entire show for free. That is unless you have a fee for the performance."

That was almost laughable. *We should pay them!*

"Well, with this great opportunity, plus the tour and show and such, we would be overpaid. We feel blessed to have been called to participate in FBN's mission. It is truly our pleasure," said Janine, "Am I speaking out of turn, ladies?"

"Janine, this is the opportunity of a lifetime. Who would have believed that after we grew old we would still have something like this poured upon us. It's come late but, believe me, not too late. I'm certainly all for it," said Anne. That was a lot for her to say, and everyone was impressed, and they agreed wholeheartedly. They could hardly contain themselves.

Bea stood up. She couldn't sit any longer. She reached out her hand to Mr. Harris and said, "Thank you so much. You have no idea what this means to me—to us!"

"You are certainly welcome. I feel that I found the best entertainment for this season."

"When are we to go?"

"We're looking at the week of August 10. It will be hot in New York, but the tour bus is air conditioned as are all the buildings. You won't be walking outdoors much unless there is something important I've left out."

"I was wondering if we would be able to get a glimpse of the Statue of Liberty?" asked Julia.

"I'll check that out for you. Some of the tours take you down far enough in the harbor to see her. I think if we were to actually go out to Staten Island, we would need another entire day, but it might be possible to include that in your tour. Don't worry. I'll follow through and let you know."

"Oh, please, no. You have done enough for us already. Don't make this some priority of yours. I'm really sorry to have brought it up," Julia said.

"That's just fine. It just might work out well, but if not, I'll tell you that also. I'm happy to look into that for you."

"All right, but please don't fuss over this. It was just something I thought up."

"Okay, I promise."

"Anybody else?"

"I know that word is going to get out, and there is going to be lots of talk around these parts about us doing this. Should we keep it quiet as much as possible, or is it good publicity to let it be known through any of the media that asks us?" asked Janine.

"Publicity is what we want. We want everyone to watch the broadcast, and we will be publicizing it ourselves as well, so brace yourselves. This could turn out to be a real attention-getter throughout the area."

"If so, I hope it is the Lord's will," said Janine.

"We at the station believe in what we are doing, Mrs. Stephens. We have had a good deal of experience with our programming. I think your group is going to spread the love of the Lord and bring much encouragement to people you cannot reach here. You are doing such a good job of it, and we are pleased to assist is a larger way."

The meeting went fabulously well. Everyone was excited and eager to make plans to go to New York. The ladies talked together after Mr. Harris left and decided upon drivers for their next local appointment. They didn't rehearse because they felt fairly drained of energy after the business meeting of the morning.

Pastor Dan left with Mr. Harris and walked him to his car.

"Mr. Harris, thank you for everything. I am so happy for our dear ladies. I would never have dreamed of anything like this coming their way. They deserve it. They've lived such good lives, been faithful servants of the Lord, and have had very few days of exciting, interesting moments above and beyond their own deliverances. We love them here at Hope Church and will be supporting their efforts both here and as they travel afar."

"It's my pleasure, Pastor. I have a great job. God is good."

"All the time!" responded Dan.

30

Ring, Ring

That afternoon and the next day, the ladies were either dialing their telephones or the phones were ringing. Word traveled fast.

Anne called her dear friend of many years, Jane.

"Hello, Jane, it's Anne."

"Oh, I know. I recognize your voice. How are you, Anne? Is everything all right?"

"Yes, everything certainly is all right. Owen's health has improved some, I'm feeling well, and something very interesting is happening that is now bringing excitement and joy into my life. I thought you would like to know about it."

"Yes, I would. We've always shared everything, both good and bad. It's great to hear something good is going on."

"Well, I've told you all about our kitchen band—and by the way, we don't call ourselves the Kitchen Band anymore. We decided we are The Band of Hope."

"I like that!"

"I do too. It means so much. First of all, this band has brought those of us who are enjoying participation within it hopefulness for a brighter future. The band is carrying hope into the world also. And the band comes from West Hope. I don't know why we didn't think of this sooner."

"That's perfect!"

"Well, wait until you hear what's coming up now. The band will be broadcast all across the nation through Faith Broadcasting Network, and we are going to New York City to FBN and do our skit there before a live audience."

"My heavens! I never would have thought that could be."

"I know. That's what we say too. It's another gift from the Lord, Jane. He has been so good to us."

"Anne, will you have the opportunity to share your story on that show? That's the main thing, I would say. The fact that God called you to do something so outrageously unheard of, and your message is reaching others who need help. I think about the times you have been to nursing homes and seen the desperate folks there smile and sing along with you. And also even sharing what you do with others in good health in churches and so forth, who can see the joy in you as you serve the Lord by bringing joy to others. You just have to get that message across."

"Mr. Harris, the main contact with FBN has been to West Hope to talk with us. He is also of that same opinion. That's what he wants. He wants more people to learn something from us."

"I say, this is the best news I've heard in a long time. When is the show going to be broadcast?"

"We will do it the week of August 10."

"Well, I'll be watching and also passing the word to everyone in my church and neighborhood."

They continued the conversation at length as Jane wanted to know all about the plans for the trip.

"Hello!"

"Hello, Ron." Bea was calling her son.

"Mother! Hi, how are you?"

"I'm just great. I have some news."

"Good news, I hope. Are you coming for Easter after all?"

"Actually, I can't. I have too much to do."

"I can't believe that. Come on, what do you have to do that's so important?"

"I'm taking a trip to New York City!"

Well, Ron was flabbergasted, of course. He's not even sure he believed what he heard.

"New York City? What's this about?"

Bea was so excited, and she emphasized how great The Band of Hope now was, how popular it was, all the good they tried to do, and the fact that Mr. Harris came and talked with them.

"Mom, wait a minute. Wait just a minute here. This could be a Ponzi scheme. Don't fall for something like this."

"What's that you're talking about?"

"That's when some fraudulent person is taking your money by making you believe something that's simply not true. Lots of people fall for their sweet talks."

"Ron, this is not a Possie scheme or whatever you call it. It's the truth."

"Who is this guy?"

"He is one of the higher-ups at the Faith Broadcasting Network."

"Has anyone checked him out?"

"Ron, this is for real. He has met with Pastor Dan, Janine, Dr. Ruth Reimer of the church regional office, and he is for real."

"Give me this man's name."

"It's Charles Harris."

"Well, hold on. Don't sign anything. I'm going to check him out and call you back. You just can't trust anybody these days."

"For heaven's sake, Ron, can't you even let me be happy?"

Bea was disturbed that he would think such a thing. She understood, and if he found out he was right, they wouldn't get to go. Now her happiness was sinking into the sand. Why couldn't he just say something to encourage her?

"I'm sorry, Mom. It's for your own good. I don't want to upset you. I'll check this out right now and get back to you. Please don't be angry."

"Okay, do what you are going to do."

With that, she hung up the phone.

Now why did he have to spoil my day like that? He could have told me he was happy for me and, without saying anything to me, make the call and check things out and call me later if he found out something bad about Mr. Harris.

He's not going to. I believe everything is going to be fine . . . I think.

Marcia called her children, who all were excited about this new adventure for their mother. They were surprised at first that she was a member of The Band of Hope and thought even that was a good thing for her to do. The trip was the cherry on top, as far as they could see.

Iola needed to look up a telephone number. It took a long time because she didn't have the phone book for Innesport. She finally followed the directions for inquiries concerning out-of-town numbers and located the one she needed.

"Hello!"

"Hello, is this Susie's Wigs?"

"Yes, it is."

"Well, I need to get fitted with a wig right away. When can I come in?"

"When will it be convenient?"

"I'm pretty free most of the time, and I am not sick or anything like that."

"Well, that's good. I'm glad to hear it. Could you come in tomorrow?"

"Yes, that would be great. What time?"

"Around 11:00 a.m.?"

"Yes. This is Iola MacCowan. I'm from West Hope."

"Okay, Mrs. MacCowan. I'll see you tomorrow. Could you give me your phone number, please?"

She made it short and sweet. She was nervous, but more than that, she was apprehensive about the reactions of others. *Well, they'll have to just get over seeing me with hair once again. After all, I'm going to New York. I can't go with my hair like this.*

Janine and John talked for a long time about every aspect of such an undertaking. They were both excited for the band.

"I'm going to call Kathy," Janine said.

Granddaughter Karen, answered the telephone.

"Hi, Karen. What's going on at your house?"

"Pretty much the same as usual. I have a lot of homework these days. School is winding down for the year and for me forever here. Oh, and guess what?"

"What?"

"Tony's going to be home from college for the weekend, and he's coming over. We may go to a movie or something as well."

"I really like that boy. He is so sweet."

"Me too."

"Did you want to talk with Mom?"

"Yes, please."

"Hi, Mom. How are you today?" asked Kathy.

"I'm feeling great. I want to share something with you."

It used to be that every time Janine talked with Kathy about something big, Kathy would be cautioning her not to overdo, but she gave up on that when the Kitchen Band got going and she saw how invigorated the members were—and most of them were far older than Janine.

Janine told Kathy all about the upcoming event and trip, and she was thrilled.

"Mom, I have known for quite some time now that your belief in the calling of the band by the Lord is real, so I believe this too. God sees everything that we can't. He will be with you, I'm sure, and it will be the experience of a lifetime. Good for you."

Janine told Deborah too. Of course, Deb is so wrapped up in her world of twin-rific that she doesn't find much room for worrying. She loved the idea and believed it was a good thing.

Harry would be told at Eastertime. That's soon enough. Janine was now exhausted with the talking and with the thoughts floating through her head.

"I need a nap," John heard her say, and he agreed that she should go tuck in and rest awhile.

Some band members were napping too or talking on the telephone. Pauline was going through her closet and looking at her clothes, wondering what she should wear in the middle of the summer in New York.

New York. Aha! What a beautiful thought. I haven't shopped for pretty things in a long, long time. I should go shopping to see the latest styles and see if I can find something new to wear."

Julia was a very quiet person with usually little to say. But at the moment, she wished she had someone to say something to. Her best friends now were the band members, and they had fairly talked themselves out today.

Her children were so distant from who she really was now that they would not have the slightest idea how to comment on her situation. All they did was fuss around maybe twice a year and then get on to their own homes again. They didn't even live close enough to come any more often than that.

I don't care. I've gotten over it. I have good friends, I have the church, I have the band, and I have a trip coming up that is going to be exciting and wonderful.

She closed her eyes and smiled while thinking good thoughts and soon was in a nice, restful sleep.

Rachael was thinking, thinking. Her creative mind was always very demanding upon her. Now she was figuring out a different hat for her country skit in the band. She had not been satisfied with her original one. After all, they were going to New York. She wanted her things shining and well chosen as best as they could be. She was thrilled when Janine asked her to bring a big broom and Janine taught her how to do pizzicato on the strings as a bass fiddle. She was getting really good at following the sound on the recording, and Janine had moved her up front and at the center of attention for the number. She didn't know one note from another, but with help, she looked like she was the best at pizzicato there could be.

She was so happy that she could walk without the cane and said a prayer to God for all the recent blessings she had. She was so near to not living through the horrible automobile accident a couple of years ago that it was a miracle that she was doing the things she could do. She was vastly grateful as she recognized that the Lord lifted her from her pain and her disabilities to be able to participate once again in the band and in life itself.

The phone rang. Bea had drifted off to a worried sleep. She reached for the phone, knocked it off, picked it up as quickly as possible, and said hello.

"Mom, it's Ron."

Oh no, my dreams are going to be totally shattered.

"Mom, are you there?"

"Yes, I'm here."

"Listen, I talked with FBN and got lots of information about Mr. Charles Harris. I am totally satisfied that this is for real. I'm sorry I caused you to feel uncomfortable and sad."

"I knew it would be fine," she said, trying to sound strong.

"Well, I just had to know. I want to tell you now that I am so happy for you. You are a born entertainer, and you'll have a lot of fun. There will be chaperones and people to see that everyone is okay at all times. I'm going to be telling everyone about the band and the trip.

When is this going to happen?"

"The week of August 10."

"Okay, that's great. I'll be up to see you before then. Will you need to go shopping for clothing or other supplies? Nancy will come with me and help you with that, if you like."

"Thank you, sweetheart. We'll see. Are you okay with all this, then?"

"Yes, Mom, I am."

"Okay, I'll be talking with you."

"Okay, bye."

"Bye."

Bea was so relieved. She didn't like having her son question this great opportunity, but since he had to do it, she now felt 100% sure of everything.

So all is well. I feel like dancing.

31

Working Hands

Pastor Dan went to call on Iola. He had some news about Jimmy Adams and his sister, Sally. The Young Marrieds had taken on the outreach project of seeing that those young folks were fed, clothed, and kept warm, at least until their mother could return to the house. Dan's efforts enlightened him as to the cause of Mrs. Adams's illness. It seemed she was under-nourished, dehydrated, and finally acquired pneumonia; however, she had recovered and was now back in her home with the children.

Iola was pleased to learn of this.

"Is the outreach going to continue?" she asked.

"Some are talking with Mrs. Adams about that. She has said that the children want to attend the Christian Fellowship for Teens. Jimmy can go too, but there is a younger group. Either way, he is on the borderline age, and if he would feel more comfortable with his sister's group, no one will argue that."

"We are hoping that they will come and learn about the goodness of the Lord, and perhaps even the day will come when their mother will want to attend West Hope Church. She is mighty poor but does clean houses, and the Young Marrieds have put out the word to call upon her for that sort of help if they need anyone."

"Well, coincidentally, I'm looking for some help around here. My wonderful, wonderful young woman who used to be available any time has gone to work in Innesport on a full-time basis. Would you want to ask her to call me if she is interested, or should I call her myself?"

"I'll talk with her about that. I'm sure she will be happy about working here. This is the way of the greater Christian family. We work together for the good of all. Sometimes it just takes an occasion such as we've experienced here, to put someone to work, to find friendship for children and help for all. It's the way it's supposed to be."

"I was a part of a working group in the church for many years. It was a pleasure. Now that I'm too old, I am delighted and encouraged to know that we have once again an energetic and vital group that is interested in helping others."

So Hope Church continued to spread the love of the Lord, raising hope for all ages: from children, through adults, and on to the elder members of the church. Also, the outreach of hope was gaining ground in many directions. The church would remain because it was finding work as the hands and feet of the Lord. As Pastor said, "We are the workers of the Kingdom. Pray for the Lord to lead us where He wants us to go, and without hesitation, go forth and do it!"

32

Sunshine and Daffodils

Harry and family were coming today! Everyone was excited. Janine had daffodils all over the house, and sunshine was not only in the sky but in the hearts of the family. Janine couldn't resist sitting down at the piano and playing that old hymn. "There is sunshine in my soul today, all glorious and bright." *These old hymns surely do have a way of saying it right.*

Yesterday when Janine visited Julia for her weekly piano lessons, Julia said that she had something special lined up for them to do after practice if she could take an extra half hour.

"What is it, Julia?" Janine was very curious because when Julia took her anywhere, she learned things that have given her great pleasure.

Julia smiled a coy smile and said, "Not yet. You'll see!"

So they finished the lesson, and instead of sitting and chatting for a while, got into Janine's car and headed out of town at Julia's direction.

It wasn't much of a drive when Julia said "Pull over here!"

There was a basket of fresh daffodils hanging on the mailbox. *How quaint.*

A lady came from around the side of the house and met them at the car. She was wearing a simple faded cotton dress, with her blond hair pinned up and sandals on her feet. She beckoned to them to come with her to the back side of the house. Janine was extremely curious. She wasn't introduced yet to the woman, and no conversation ensued.

When they came to the back of the house, a marvelous thing happened! Suddenly there before their eyes were thousands of daffodils in shades from near white, through the traditional yellow, to almost orange—but mostly bright yellow! Thousands! There were butterflies delightfully floating over and into the flowers. This scene could not be captured for still life, for the fluttering wings of the butterflies and the gentle swaying of some of the daffodils were unquestionably in a breathing garden of life.

Janine just stood there transfixed. She took Julia's hand, showing her appreciation without speaking. She had never ever seen such a full field of daffodils or any other flower.

The woman stood watching Janine. This was the old, old story. Everyone who ever came in the spring during daffodil days had the very same reaction.

Janine finally spoke. "Oh my goodness! How beautiful. I cannot believe my eyes!"

They moved forward, and the delicate fragrance of the lovely flowers swirled around them. Soon she noticed a little pathway through the thousands. The lady led them through and Julia and Janine followed. They came to a small cleared section where there was placed an adorable wood bench. They stopped, surrounded by the daffodils, all raising their heads to the source of their life and strength. The lady turned to Janine and extended her hand and said, "I'm Norah Cleary, and I'm 'appy to 'ave ya cume."

"Thank you, Norah. I'm Janine Stephens. I had no idea I would see such a impressive array of daffodils here or anywhere. Who is responsible for this lovely garden?"

"Well, when me family came over from Ireland, they moved to this area. Me Da and Mum built here, and Mum was so very fond of flowers that she straight away began the plantin' of 'em. It turned out that she took pleasure in the daffodils and started on gatherin' up the bulbs each year and spreadin' them all around. Me parents are gone now, and bein' unmarried, I have placed me heart into keepin' the garden and carin' for it and probably will do so until the end when I lay down me head."

"How lovely. You have such a fine talent for gardening. How many different varieties of daffodils are here?"

"Well, I dunno for certain, but could be forty or so. There are many others that I've not gotten yet."

Janine noticed some of the yellows had deep-orange centers, some had white, some were all yellow, and there were different sizes. She never knew!

They sat on the bench and just stayed there, quietly taking in the beauty and the fragrances. Norah said that she wanted to give her a basket of them and asked if she had a preference.

"Oh my, no! I think they are all so beautiful. Wherever you feel you can easily pick is perfect."

So Norah went about, lovingly picking her precious daffodils for the joy of giving. She had perhaps fifty of them in a lovely basket that she placed in Janine's arms.

"It pleasures me to give these to you. I also want to give you the basket. You 'ave made me 'appy today by the look on yer face. Enjoy these at your home."

"Well, thank you so much! You are overwhelming me with your kindness and generosity. My son is travelling to my home tomorrow from Oklahoma, and I will place these around the house to bring the sunshine further in."

They walked around the house, and Janine had to wipe a tear from her eye. She was so moved by the beauty of the flowers and the beauty of the one who cared for them. What a gift!

They left with their good-byes, and Janine knew she had been blessed by the occasion.

Once again as Janine was driving home from her visit with Julia with another of her gifts to her, she was filled with joyful emotion.

"Thank you, Lord, for Julia and her desire to see me happy. She is a precious part of this new life You have given to me. I can almost picture You placing people in my path. It is so clear to me. Thank You, thank You. I can never be worthy of all that I receive from You."

Janine enjoyed separating the daffodils—a symbol of hope in season—and putting them in vases throughout the house. What a perfect touch of welcome for her family.

33

Harry Is Here!

Here they are! Janine and John heard the SUV and saw the headlights coming in the driveway. They went out the front door to greet them. William, the oldest boy, got to them first. He was stronger and apparently pretty fast as well.

Granddad got the first hug. Next was Charles, the second child, followed by James. They all hugged in turn and hugged Grandma too. *Mmmm, hugs are great,* Grandma was thinking. She was so sentimental that she had to force herself not to cry when holding onto her dear grandsons.

My life is good. If I could change anything, it would be to have all my children near to me. It is so sad not to watch these dear ones growing day by day. I must stop with this thought right now. I have them here, don't I? I'm grateful to have them here right now!

She loved her grandchildren, but no one meant more than her own dear son, Harry. He came up onto the stoop and practically swept Janine off her feet and held on with the best bear hug in the world. Janine was floating with happiness.

Of course, next was Rhonda. It was sweet of her to let the guys rush up like they did. She was happy for them all and understood. Janine and John welcomed her with a kiss and hugs. They left the luggage for the time being and all went on into the house.

Harry was so interested in the layout of the rooms, the big living room, the very nice kitchen—everything. He showed the boys the downstairs, which Janine and John had turned into a man cave for them. The guys were happy and loved having the area to themselves too.

Janine had baked pies for them, which they wanted immediately. So they all sat down to pie and ice cream and talked about everything.

The boys wanted to know when they could go see the little babies.

"Tomorrow. Aunt Deb is expecting us all tomorrow. You are going to love the little ones. They are so cute. They really don't do much yet but eat and sleep and smile."

"That's okay, we still want to see them," said Charles.

"I think Kathy and her family will be over soon. They wanted to see you tonight and not wait until morning."

At that, a barking was heard. Everyone was alerted to it. Years ago, when Prince was a tiny little puppy, the boys visited with Aunt Kathy and enjoyed Prince so much. They were going to be surprised to see a dog almost as big as they were.

Karen, Meghan, and Prince all got out of the SUV together, and Prince ran to the door. The boys didn't realize that he was at the door when they ran to it to open it. But there he was, a very big dog, and they were startled! Grandma said, "Don't worry. He will just want to smell you, and he will love you."

Well, she was right, of course.

Here are little people. I don't know them, but they look like good ones to be with. I'll just sit here and smell them. Hmm, they seem fine. They want to get closer, and that's good.

Prince was accepting the boys without any problem, and that's exactly what everyone expected. Before anyone knew it, the boys were on the floor with him and all were rolling in one big lump. The boys and the dog were going to be super friends.

Kathy came through the door, looking for her brother. When she found him, she wrapped her arms around him and had no intention of letting go for a while. Harry felt the same, so that was all about family waiting and loving.

Kathy hugged Rhonda too, and she went for a cup of coffee and sat at the table while the guys and the dog and Greg went downstairs for a little while. Harry stayed with his sister while they talked about the house their parents had now, his house and property that were constantly being reworked, and life in Oklahoma with all its unexpected weather conditions.

Harry slipped away eventually and joined the fun downstairs for a while.

"Wow! Prince, boy, you have grown into quite a handsome fellow!"

Prince sat down and looked into Harry's eyes and touched his nose to his hand. Harry petted him and rubbed him, and Prince was totally satisfied that these people are just fine with him.

The boys showed Harry that the refrigerator was stocked with healthy foods and that they also had a bathroom of their own downstairs. "And look at the big-screen television!"

Oh boy, they were going to be very satisfied with their arrangements at Grandma's house.

Harry and Greg went back upstairs and left the boys and the dog to relax as they saw fit.

"Harry, how do you like Oklahoma?" asked Greg.

"You know, it's fine most of the time. The neighbors and residents, in general, enjoy the basics of life. They are friendly—the salt of the earth, so to speak, but I can never predict the weather. It is always extreme, no matter if it's heat, rain, wind, or snow. I don't know if I ever will adjust to all of it, but I do like my job, and our home is shaping up to be very comfortable for us. Rhonda loves it there and has a lot of friends, so we will continue on there and work against the elements as we have to. I'll tell you—the tornadoes last summer almost drove us out."

"We lost friends in it, you know, and saw many homes down. It took all of the neighborhood working together to bring life back into some of the areas. I understand what Harry is saying, but home is home, you know. Nothing is perfect in this world. We have to make our world as much our own as we can. We're doing well," said Rhonda.

"Yep! And the boys love it there. It's the only life they've ever known. I think we're there to stay as long as my job continues to be fulfilling and pays the bills."

"I always miss the NFL football games that we used to see here in the East, especially the Steelers, but we catch them on television once in a while. I make a pretty big deal of that with the boys, so now they are fans too. I think we'll try to get over to Pittsburgh and let them see the stadium if possible, and the rivers. We might get here for a real game next year. I'm planning on that."

Janine jumped at that statement. "Christmas! Oh, wouldn't that be just wonderful?"

"It would, Mom, it would. We'll see."

"Of course, out West we are really into rodeos. That is a lot of fun. I would never encourage the boys to ride a bucking horse, though. They do get lots of exercise at school with soccer, baseball, some football, and basketball. The good exercise helps to keep them fit, and they love to participate. So there are lots of things to do. We all ride horses."

Kathy's girls were smiling at that. "We love horses too."

"I want to be a professional rider. I train with my neighbors," said Meghan.

"Well, you and William need to talk together about horses. That's his main thought these days. How about that? You are worlds apart and yet have the same interest."

34

Rejoice

Janine enjoyed Easter music because it was over-expressive for the Risen Lord, and usually, the music was meant to be loud. If not, she made it so! *After all, why are we here on this particular Sunday? Let's grasp the opportunity to praise and rejoice that Christ is risen.*

Church attendance was down considerably during the bleak winter Sundays, and some people seemed to get away from the practice of regular weekly attendance for worship but never on Easter Sunday. Janine enjoyed seeing the pews nearly full. Her family sat all together in two rows. There was Deborah, Robert, and the dear, darling twin girls who were going to be baptized today. In the same row sat Robert's parents and his brother and his wife. The other row held Harry, Rhonda, and the three boys along with Kathy, Greg, and their two daughters, all a little squeezed, but they would not have it any other way.

Of course, John was in the choir, and Janine was playing her joyful heart out. It was a wonderful occasion.

When Pastor Dan invited the family to join in the baptism, all of them came forward to be close. John left the choir to stand right beside his daughter and, on this rare and special occasion, Janine left her position at the organ and stood beside John and was extremely happy to have her family members all together. A picture of the family was taken by someone in the congregation, and Janine wondered who took it and hoped that whoever it was would be giving a copy to her.

Everyone looked spiffy. Even the boys had new suits and western ties. It was a picture for sure.

The babies were in beautiful long baptismal dresses and had little flowered headbands on. *My goodness! How wonderful.*

Little Annette was fine and curious with the water on her head, but Annabelle reacted to the unexpected action by fussing in her daddy's arms, but only for a moment—then all was well. The little boys were tickled over it all.

Pastor Dan made a practice of carrying a newly baptized baby up and down the pews throughout the congregation, following the ceremony, and Janine wondered if he would carry two at the same time today. He was a strong and fit fellow, and with a baby in each arm, he bravely and happily introduced the babies to all members of the church. Janine continued to stand with the family even though she usually played a lovely tune during that time. The scene was complete without it. No music was needed.

Grandma was not going to cook today. She enjoyed having the family all around the tables together and preparing meals most of the time; however, today they were returning to Kathy and Greg's because Greg had insisted upon doing the honors.

No one would ever complain about that! And won't Prince be glad?

They all arrived in their small caravan to the house in a convoy. Janine and John drove their own car because the babies and all the equipment fairly well filled the Franklins' car, and Harry and his family came along in the rental, except for James who really, really wanted to ride with the babies. Deborah arranged it well, and off they went.

Greg had started the dinner in the middle of the night and had prepared salads the day before. He was very organized and a great cook. The house was full of the fragrance of roast pork seasoned with herbs according to Greg's way. He went directly into the kitchen and opened the oven door, and more titillating aromas drifted out. Checking with a fork, he found the roast perfectly ready. The vegetables were all in a great Crock-Pot and would be dished out with the roast.

Greg and his family had put up the tables out in the great room last night, and the places were set. How nice they looked! It was an occasion, and his daughters once again jumped in with fancy decorations they found from the internet. They said that all they had to do was print them out and cut them. The theme was baby girls, all in pastels. They were going to do pink, but Kathy thought the boys would prefer not to sit at a pink table. Ha! That was probably good thinking!

Janine ordered flowers for the tables. She arranged them in small low bouquets and put them in the car this morning. She could have still used some of the daffodils, but they had served their purpose well and could just stay home for another day.

Saturday, Rhonda made a beautiful cake for the dinner. She had recently taken cake-decorating classes and put those skills to good use. She said with all the cakes and occasions for her boys, she figured she had better learn the decorating skills and save some money. She learned well. The cake could have come from one of the bakeries. Harry was impressed, and that pleased Rhonda even more.

John said grace before the meal, and he had so much to thank God for that the family was getting jittery. Greg expected it and didn't put the hot foods on the table until Granddad was finished with the lengthy—but important—prayer.

Oh, yum! One dish at a time was passed around the crowd. They all ate their fill, except the little babies who were sound asleep throughout dinner. Prince was a prince by keeping out of the way and curling up in front of the banked fireplace. Just a little warmth was coming into the room, and it was as cozy as could be. Janine was thinking that this occasion was one of those to squirrel away into memory for the rest of her life, and the pictures taken today would certainly authenticate with accuracy the beauty of it from the heart, mind, and spirit.

ϓϓϓ

Harry and Janine were the last two to go to bed that night. They liked it that way because there had not been time for a quiet conversation since Harry had arrived, and the time had ended because he would be leaving tomorrow to go back to his home in Oklahoma.

"Mom, this has been a wonderful visit for all of us. I'm sorry we couldn't stay a longer time, but you know how it is with school children and gratefully employed adults as well.

"We will always remember being here and the warm gatherings together with all the family. And I'm glad that the boys have found out once again what wonderful grandparents they have here. They will want to come back real soon, and I'll see what I can do to make that happen."

"Good. And we'll see you in Oklahoma in September or October, I think. We've been planning that, and unless something gets in the way, that is still on our to-do list."

"Well, with the New York City trip coming up, you'll have to forget anything else for the time being. Just enjoy the planning for the Kitchen Band ladies and the practices and have a wonderful time there. It will be so great. How many groups of this age would ever make such plans? I'd say maybe none. It will work out just fine because it is meant to be."

"Yes, I know."

He took his mother's hands.

"Mom, I want to tell you face-to-face how much I appreciate you and all that you have sacrificed while I was a boy to see that I grew up learning what was right and wrong. Sometimes I thought all that talk was stiffening and not the life I would want to live, and when I got away on my own, I'd do what I really wanted to do. But here's the truth: I never wanted to do those things I had thought about doing, because when I was an adult, I finally recognized for myself—due to all the right upbringing lessons—that what I really wanted was to live life according to the way I always did and to be a good parent like you and Dad.

"More and more in various circumstances, I have found myself making decisions in the ways that I think you and Dad would do."

"Harry, that's what every parent would want to hear. Thank you for taking the time to sit down and say it, but I could tell that you were bringing your boys up right anyway."

"Maybe my little guys will see through the smokescreens of life also and will turn out to be happy doing things the right way."

"They will."

She quietly slipped into bed, stared straight up at the ceiling and recalled word-for-word the conversation of this evening and other parts of the recent visit. She was so happy with her family. Some parents hadn't been so fortunate, and Janine felt remorse and sorrow for them. It's much easier to bring children through the experimental and changing seasons of their lives when home life was strong and both parents were striving together to teach their children the good they should do. Two standing together made the effort much easier and probably more successful. Janine said a prayer for all those who were struggling against great odds in the world without support.

John was not asleep as she thought. When she calmed herself down and turned over on her side, he was right behind her, pulling her to him in their comfort zones. Who could ask for anything more?

35

Get Ready

The ladies of The Band of Hope were extremely hopeful these days. They had talked things over, and everything was pretty well determined about the trip to NYC.

The Faith Broadcasting Network had notified the Pittsburgh newspaper that first printed the story about The Band of Hope that the ladies were now going to be on live television. It only seemed right that the newspaper would get the first scoop on it all. Naturally, the reporter called Janine and suggested that he come to West Hope and talk with the ladies in costume, take a few pictures, and tell everyone about the trip they were going to take. So right away, the reporter put in another great article about the band.

Iola was so glad that she had her new wig to wear for the picture. It was taking a bit of time to adjust to wearing it, but the band members thought she looked really nice, and that helped.

The next performance they had was in another senior center, but this time it was a bit closer to home, which was nice because some of the band members and the residents knew one another from years gone by. It turned out to be a really good day. The social director welcomed the band immediately and told them that she was really excited about their trip. Everyone was talking about it, and the residents would probably ask them some questions.

They sure did. But the band members gently broke up the conversations and slipped into their routine easily. After the program was over, they talked with the audience about their excitement and about some of the things they would be doing in New York City. Some wanted them to go entertaining to other places in the immediate area so that this friend and that friend could get to meet them.

Janine could see that things were going to get out of hand if they weren't careful. When some in the audience were asking for their business cards, the ladies had to say that they were actually booked up until August now. Who would have ever guessed that? They had to turn down invitations. They really didn't want to and could possibly try to accommodate at a later date those who had to be passed over right now. The ladies of the band surely were in high spirits. Everywhere they went, people were asking them how they felt about being recognized by a national television network, how they were going to get there, when the show would be televised, etc. It was all good, though, and each member seemed to be stronger and stronger each day as they prepared for the trip.

Actually, unknown to anyone else, Bea was not well for a short period of time and cancelled participation with an excuse of another appointment. She did not want to be sick! She did not want to have anyone fuss over her either, so she brushed it all off and was ready and raring to go the next time.

Janine asked each one of them to try to walk more or exercise according to what they could to build up some extra stamina. Some had indoor walkers and would be getting on them every day. Anne had always walked outside, and with the weather improving day by day, she would be walking as usual.

Bea worked in her flower gardens a lot. That was good exercise. Her famous yellow irises were budding. The entire neighborhood looked forward to the rows of irises on both sides of her driveway.

Iola bought an exercise bicycle, had it delivered, and used it as she could. She always did workouts with the television as well. She was determined to stay fit.

Julia didn't move around a whole lot. At ninety-one years old, she was the oldest member of the band. She felt better than she would have expected to feel at her age, still took piano lessons, had to climb up a flight to the second floor of her house, and attended church every Sunday possible. She hoped she would be able to keep up in New York City. She was sure not going to give up. To her, this was like reaching for the ring and grabbing it. She *would* be fine.

Pauline found in her apartment a fine place for walking. The hallways are long, and she could walk through the halls many times without fear of falling. She counted the times and improved each week. Otherwise, she was on that boring walker in her living room.

Rachael was continuing what she had done all winter with walking—only, she was adding more times around the rooms. She had a fear of going outside alone, and Albert has cautioned her to be extremely careful on grass and uneven ground.

Marcia was so excited over everything. She loved being in the band. She was always coming up with interesting things to present or say, and she was a worker with lots of energy and strength from the orchard to the restaurant. She rarely sat down.

Janine was busy also, but realized that walking was really her thing. She is out every morning if it isn't raining. She did not want to catch a cold, so she avoided getting wet or chilled. Her normal walking route took her past some neighbors, and she looked for them to speak to. She had especially enjoyed conversations with Abraham and Sarah at the farmhouse. She had learned new and interesting things from them about farming and surviving, and in general, she enjoyed them for their steadfastness and permanency in the face of difficulties.

These who have lived through so much but still have hope for the future are worthy of our attention, and these beautiful people can tell stories like no one else. I'm honored to know them.

36

Going to the County Fair

Under the Big Tent: The Band of Hope—1:00 p.m.—Monday

This was the final appearance of the band before leaving for the trip to New York. It was their second year to be invited to entertain the happy and boisterous fair-going crowd. Last year, about 150 older folks sat in on the action. They loved the show. They applauded and carried on, and the band had a wonderful time. It was hot, but the event planner had the foresight to have a really big fan blowing toward the ladies, and they handled it well.

When they arrived at the grounds, there were, as usual, volunteers driving open-seated vehicles to take folks to any area of the fair that they preferred. Today, they were immediately recognized by the drivers.

"Well, here are those famous ladies of the band."

"Hello, ladies, I guess you're going to the big tent today."

"We have driven a lot of people up to the tent who are just itching to see you today."

"You're looking lovely. Have fun today."

"Hey, come ride with me. I'm stopping at the big tent."

The ladies were bubbling with excitement. Life had taken a turn for the better by far. No more sitting at home, drifting off to sleep, wondering what to do to fill the time. No sirree! They were full of energy and excitement and ready to go at any moment.

The drivers all got out of the rovers and lifted the bags of instruments up to the stage for them. There was always a sense of the right way to do things here at the fair—back to basics and down to individual politeness.

They found themselves on the big stage, facing perhaps four hundred people! They were calling out to the ladies, clapping for encouragement even as they were still setting up for the performance. Joy was in the air. The ladies picked up on it all and gave a great performance, inviting people to come on stage and participate now and then, and laughing with them throughout.

Bea came carrying a splatter shield that prevented grease from splashing out on a stove when browning meat or other foods. It was fancied up with ribbons. Janine asked her during the performance what it was, and she said it was a "Splattervarius." Janine almost fell over with laughter, and everyone else reacted just the way Bea expected.

Yes, a Splattervarius violin—which she played very properly in the "Edelweiss" routine. It would hopefully go into the part that would be chosen for presentation that coming week. Bea was a real crackerjack. Everyone loved having her around, and everyone enjoyed her playfulness and her lively spirit. Thankfully she was feeling well today. She had not spoken to anyone about her recent health issues because she did not want anything to said about her staying home from the trip.

This is my time. This is my time to really do something big and special, and I don't want to be held back. I'll be fine. I feel good today.

What a great day they had! The audience lingered to speak one-on-one with those in the band they knew, and even strangers had come and wish them well in the upcoming venture.

ᘛᘛᘛ

With all the fuss throughout the area that The Band of Hope was going to be on national television, most of the folks who had already had the joy of being in their audience were not surprised. They had passed the word about the band, which had been the process for the band's success. No advertisements had been issued, no telephone calls from the band or Janine to organizations had ever taken place, and yet by word of mouth, they had entertained at hundreds of places, mostly within a thirty-five-mile radius—some over and over again. Janine had calculated that perhaps more than four thousand people had already seen the band in action.

37

Get Set

The Church at West Hope wanted to do something special for the band, and it was decided to have a fellowship dinner after church the Sunday before they were to leave. The ladies were told not to fix anything. Imagine that! There they were with those who meant the most to them. That in itself was a great privilege. Of course, the food was as delicious as the folks at West Hope Church were known to provide.

The social committee had creative talent above and beyond the ordinary for any occasion. Today they had signposts that read "New York" and "FBN" and "Queen Isabel Hotel" pointing the way to the fellowship hall. There were bright lights shining here and there in the dining room area, and it felt as though they were walking into a completely different place with all their friends there with them.

The tables were decorated with little suitcases overflowing with toy instruments.

The choir had prepared a couple of fun songs to sing to them. This was also a rare treat for the congregation, as they were a very serious choir, always focusing upon the music for a worshipping people. Someone had written funny words to old tunes, and they had a sing-along that Janine had nothing to do with. She enjoyed herself to the greatest extent.

After dinner, Pastor Dan spoke for the congregation, wishing them a safe and satisfactory trip. And, of all things, they were presented with pull-along suitcases, each in a different color or pattern! What a terrific surprise! They had to go home and repack!

Before they all went out of the building, Pastor Dan led the congregation in a prayer that what they do and say would bring others to a new awareness of possibilities of sharing the love of the Lord. He prayed for their good health, their safety, and for them to have a wonderful time of it.

Hugs and expressions of love were shared with the church family. The ladies felt the love and knew that they were a part of something very special.

The ladies of the band went outside with their pull-alongs, waving good-bye. Cameras were busy, and a picture would certainly be posted on the bulletin board when they return.

ᕗᕗᕗ

Janine was alone at the moment and enjoying a little time for reflection. She sat down on the sofa in her living room and let her mind wander where it wanted to go.

People would say this is unbelievable. Old ladies, fairly well-adjusted to just sitting back and letting the days pass over them have come alive again, enjoying something new.

There's the key! We get so used to doldrums that we settle for that and decide it is just the way it is going to be.

This is the Lord's will. It has been from the day I walked into their Sunday school room and practically made a confusing mess of suggesting they get together and start up a kitchen band. I know the Lord sent me, but I didn't do my part well. I was not adequately prepared. I fumbled through the entire conversation.

Suddenly, dear loving and quiet Julia stepped forward in my defense and agreed to try my suggestion. If it had collapsed before it got started, it would have been my fault and mine alone.

"For you do not know the plans I have for you." I've read that scripture from Jeremiah 29 many times. Now I can see that it's true.

Looking back over my life, I'm sure I missed doing what I should have done more times than not.

His plans for His kingdom depend upon us being aware of Him. That means pulling closer, listening. Thankfully, this time I guess I did.

The band has been given a tremendous opportunity to share His blessed gifts to a mass of people tuning into the television program who will see energy and vitality coming forth from a completely improbable group who, by His grace, displays the joy that a Christian life offers.

"You do not know the plans I have for you."

Well, I would not have imagined that we would be leaving tomorrow for New York City. No way. These are not my plans at all, but I believe there is a good reason for it, and it will work out well.

People are inspired when they see The Band of Hope. It's a blessing given to us to pass along to others. We are here for a reason, and it certainly is not to find happiness within ourselves. Yet we do find overflowing joy in serving Him, which is even better than what the world has. Riches will certainly pass away, as the scriptures say. Yes, that's the truth. Our joy in the Lord is everlasting.

Sometime later she heard, "Hey, honey, are you asleep?" John was asking.

"Oh yes, I guess I dozed off. I'd better get on to bed. Tomorrow will be here before we know it."

Yes, Monday was the final day, and she would be going over and over the list that each and every member of the band had as well. Janine was sure she had it all gathered up on the bed in the spare bedroom.

Notes were everywhere. Janine felt a responsibility for the band members. She hoped no one got ill at any time during the trip and that everybody remembered everything really important.

ᵔᵔᵔ

On Monday morning, the ladies were so excited they could hardly sit still. There were many unknowns to this upcoming trip, but no one felt afraid. They believed they would have fun and that they would do well with the entertaining. They always did. Thankfully each and every one of them felt well and capable of handling the travelling.

All, that is, except Bea.

The past couple of weeks, her illness had returned, and she had known that something wasn't right with her. Bea would wake up in the mornings, feeling too tired to move, and there was a weight on her chest that seemed to hold her down.

I'm ninety years old. I've lived this long. Please, Lord, help me to live a tiny bit longer so that I can go on this trip. Also, if I don't feel well enough to go, it will spoil the trip for everyone. I don't want that to happen. It's going to be the finest thing that has happened to us all for many years, Lord.

I shouldn't ask for any more days, Lord. I don't want You to think I don't appreciate that You've given me a lot more days than I could have thought of having. I do appreciate that. It's just that this is one of those extra-special times that could ever be for old folks like us, and Lord, if You could please answer this prayer, I won't ask for another thing.

She had been almost holding her breath the last several days, wondering if she would have a heart attack. She didn't want to go to a doctor. In a little town such as hers, everyone would know that she did. First of all, she'd have to ask someone to drive her or take that slow van that picks up seniors and uses up the entire day. Either way, she would have everyone asking her about going to the doctor. So she figured that if she took it easy, took Tums for indigestion and aspirin for circulation, ate as well as she could, and prayed a lot, she'd make it.

She got up and believed that the Lord was answering her prayer. She took a deeper breath than usual, and it was fine. She tried another. No pain—so she moved along to the bathroom, went to the kitchen, and fixed her tea and toast. Hey! She felt fine!

She looked upward and said a little prayer of thanks and got on with the day.

I need to be sure I have everything, because now I can tell that I am going to go after all.

She called Pauline, and the two of them talked for forty-five minutes about all that they were going to see and do.

Pauline said she didn't want anyone handling her trombone, so she was going to carry it on.

"They won't let you do that," Bea said.

"They will. I bought a trombone case at the music store. I'll put my trombone in there. They do let you take musical instruments on. Once I saw a guitar case up front with a few other such cases, so I think it will work just fine."

Bea knew how important it was for Pauline to protect her trombone. Good heavens, no one in the band would dare touch it, so Bea hoped that it would go on the airplane just as Pauline said.

She left the telephone and went about her day smiling and had only good thoughts of her life today, tomorrow, and for the upcoming days ahead.

38

Go!

This was the day! The sky was clear; however, being in early August, the air was heavy and just too hot for comfort. By the time Janine's car was loaded with her things and she had hugged her family who came to bid her a safe and glorious trip, she was hot and thirsty. She had cold water to go and drank down half a bottle before they were out on the main road.

"Whew! What is the temperature anyway?" she asked John, who was driving.

"Says eighty-four degrees outside of the car, and it's early. Thank goodness for air conditioning."

"I know, but we planned a bus tour for today. What's the weather supposed to be in New York? Did you notice?"

"Of course. Apparently there's a nice breeze blowing from the east, and the temperature is not too bad. The humidity is lower too. So don't worry. I think you are going to be fine."

"It's not me. It's the ladies! I don't want them to have a stroke or something."

"Janine, stop that. You know it's going to be fine. You aren't even there yet. You are once more getting the cart before the horse."

"Okay, okay. You're right. It will be fine."

They picked up Rachael. Her son, Albert, and her daughter, Celeste, were at her little house on the hill to bid her farewell. There was Rachael, smiling like no other smile in the world. She was so happy, and so was her family. No one could have ever guessed that Rachael would ever have been in such good shape after the accident. But she's ready and raring to go.

John gathered up her rolling suitcase and one carry-on. Rachael obviously knew how to pack.

The family kissed and hugged her and waved at the car until they were out of sight.

Next was Julia in town. She was standing on the porch, and she had her hair curled and had nice lipstick, pretty pearls, and summer slacks on. She looked neat and ready for New York. There wasn't anyone to say good-bye to her, so the stop was short and sweet.

Conversations kept up a fast pace, and before they knew it, they were at the Pittsburgh airport. John left them out at the door, a porter was available and immediately began lifting baggage from the trunk of the car and putting everything on a cart. John knew just what to say to him. Since John was not permitted to leave his car, he quickly kissed Janine good-bye and hurried away.

She was on her own!

Showing calmness and savvy authority, she directed the ladies to come along with her, and through the doors they went, into the huge airport, and found that the porter was there waiting for them, and he took them to the counter. He was a great help, and they felt that they had known him always. They knew enough to tip him a bit. He tipped his cap to them, smiled, and bid them a safe trip.

Looking around, they right away saw Iola, Marcia, Bea, and Anne. The only one not there was Pauline. Good grief. She said she'd be fine and would just park her car in the long-term parking as she always did. She sounded as though she knew exactly what to do.

"I hope she gets here on time. What if she doesn't?" asked Julia.

"We have a lot of extra time. Don't worry. That's one of the reasons we have to always be at the airport two hours ahead of time. She knows where we are going to meet up."

"Where?" Julia asked.

Marcia said that they had arranged for everyone to just go ahead to the boarding area, and Pauline would check in and meet them there.

"Don't worry about Pauline. She wouldn't miss this trip for the world," Bea said.

Bea was as excited as anyone. She didn't have any pain today. All was well.

Julia had never flown. At first when she heard they would fly, she was all shook up about it, but no one else seemed to be worried in the least, so eventually, she just let it all go.

However, now that she was here and there were people rushing past her, it made her nervous again.

Marcia sensed her apprehension, and she put her hand on her shoulder and kept it there while they were getting in line to check in. That helped a lot! Julia calmed down.

When everyone had their boarding passes and baggage checked, Janine gathered them together.

"I want each of us to have a hand on a partner to board the transit that takes us to the other wing of the airport. So, I'll take Julia with me, Iola and Anne, and Rachel with—wait a minute. That won't work."

"I'll be fine, Janine. I know all about the security and the train. Let me be by myself, and Iola and Rachel can pair up," Anne suggested.

Iola and Rachel seemed satisfied with that, so it was affirmed.

No one thought about having to take off shoes to go through security. Most of them had on shoes that were tied. They did not bend over as well as they used to, so it was up to Marcia and Janine to help out with that. The shoes were moving along while they stood to be searched, and it was rather unnerving for them. Janine went last just to be sure they were all through.

But lo and behold, Julia was chosen to go to a separate room and be scanned.

Janine was angry about them taking Julia, and she followed right along and told them how ridiculous it was and that she wanted to speak to the one in charge.

"Madam, *I am* in charge!"

Marcia had grabbed Julia's belongings; they put her shoes on her, and Janine slid into hers and followed right smack behind Julia.

"Now, listen here. This is crazy. Look at this dear woman. She is not a security risk by any stretch of the imagination. Why don't you get someone else if you have to meet a quota?"

The security person didn't even answer Janine.

"Come on now. This doesn't hurt. We will be finished in a couple of minutes." He looked firmly at Janine. "*You* stay outside here and wait."

Julia looked timid and almost afraid. She knew she would be okay, so she just steeled herself and decided to not let him get the best of her. She stood still while the scanner went over every inch of her body, up and down and between. Good grief! But she still did not falter. She just looked ahead, put her chin up and got over it.

When she came out and passed the test, she seemed to have grown a couple of inches, and also was without a tremble or fright. She had conquered the enemy, and she was stronger for it!

Janine was amazed at her! She was ready to comfort her, and here Julia was strutting along, daring the world to come up against her. Janine would remember this occasion as long as she lived.

Everyone was ready now to go to the boarding of the train. There wasn't much to it, but Janine and Marcia would be watching every move made by their elderly friends.

All they had to do was step over the edge and into the car and sit down as soon as possible. People their age were not used to moving quickly. Gradually over the years, each person learns to take her time and not hurry. Now they *had* to do it.

The transit pulled up—*ding, ding, ding*. The doors opened wide. No steps, just move forward and step over the small, small gap between the platform and the car.

Iola and Anne went on first, very quickly; Julia was next with head high; Bea and Marcia moved on followed by Rachael; and Janine, relieved, stepped over from the platform; and they were all there!

Anyone who could give a seat to the ladies did so without hesitation, and the transit moved forward on the track and underground. Julia thought it was great, and everyone was fine with the ride.

They arrived at the other side of the huge airport to find their departure number. Without any problems, they took their time and looked all around at the many stores and all the people moving in every direction. No one chose to jump onto the moving floor. It was just too much to expect.

They had a good amount of time, so they did not have to hurry. They took in the atmosphere, and before long, they were at the seating area of their flight to New York.

Many travelers were curious about the group of ladies. They were nodding and whispering about them, wondering why they were traveling together and what adventure they might possibly be having.

The ladies were aware of their curiosity but chose not to get involved at that point. Pauline was not there. Janine tried Pauline's cell phone number but did not get through to her. Janine looked at the clock. *She still has time.*

Bea began to feel uncomfortable about Pauline. She talked with her on the phone yesterday.

There was a restroom right in the same part of the section of the seats, so the delegation at one time or other, but two by two, took advantage of that.

Everyone assumed a comfortable seated position and talked or read and worried some that Pauline was not with them.

Janine's cell phone rang.

"Hello."

"Janine, this is Pauline. Don't worry, I'm fine. I'm at the ticket counter. I had just a bit of trouble with my baggage. It's all right now. I convinced them that I had to carry my musical instrument on with me because it is one of a kind and quite valuable. They looked at it and didn't know the difference." She laughed, and so did Janine, although Janine was so relieved she really felt like crying instead.

"Okay, be careful going through security. They grabbed Julia out for scanning, for heaven's sake. Are you okay with getting on and off the transit system?"

"Yes, I know how to do that. I'll see you soon. We still have a lot of time. Is anyone hungry? I am."

"There is a real nice little sandwich shop right close to us. How about just coming here and getting something to eat? I want you right here, please."

"Oh yes, of course. No problem. I'll be there before you know it, trombone in tow."

Pauline had already been stopped at security to check out her trombone, which was permitted to remain with her. She had picked it up, and walked lickety-split away from that area on toward the transit system.

She certainly looked like a serious instrumentalist, carrying that case. She was dressed in very flattering slacks with cube-heeled beige shoes. She had a beautiful but sensible hat on her head, with a lovely pin pulling up one side of the very smart-looking brim. She was tall, held her head high, and knew she looked like a well-traveled and knowledgeable musician. She ate it up. She was at her acting best and fooled everyone.

When she arrived to join up with the delegation, everyone jumped toward her and let her know how happy they were to see her. She retained her personality for a little while, insisting that she had done this many times before and knew all the while that she would not be late. Eventually, she relaxed into her normal self, and everyone giggled with her and enjoyed her shenanigans. *Leave it to Pauline. She is one terrific actor.*

The ladies were excited when they began calling the passengers to board the airplane. They were called first by the airline agent, and the rest of the passengers stood aside for them to board. This was so much easier for them rather than to be bumped along, and they were seated near the front of the airplane, with seats together.

Surprisingly, Julia got a window seat. She didn't know if she liked that at first. She probably would be afraid to even look out, but she wasn't going to say anything. Bea was with her. Across the aisle were Rachael and Iola. Janine and Marcia were glad they were behind everyone so that they could observe the responses from the liftoff and so forth.

They were given their instructions. They all paid close attention to everything they were told, of course, especially about the life jackets and the oxygen tanks. One never knows.

At takeoff, everyone quieted down. Julia was saying a silent prayer and figured everyone else was too. If so, they should be fine, she figured. She looked out the window and noticed that even though she couldn't tell, the airplane was moving along on the runway. They turned left. They stopped. They stayed that way. *Now what?*

She soon found out! There was a mighty roar—really loud! The airplane was revving up and shaking a bit. She didn't know if everything was all right or not. She looked at some of the others. They were very casual about it all, so she decided it must be normal and okay. Next thing she knew, the airplane was moving with an even louder noise. It got really loud, and when she looked out the window again, she saw that they were off the ground! Oh my! Then she couldn't see anything as they were in the clouds. Oh my! She didn't know if she should look again, but she couldn't resist, so she turned her head to the window and saw that the plane was tipped over to her side, and she was looking down on the clouds and could see through a bit at some of the ground and little tiny buildings below. Oh my! The airplane straightened up and began heading in one direction yet higher. Okay!

She felt a little better because everyone said that the takeoff and landing were the most scary times. She would settle back a bit and loosen up her arms that had been hugging her during takeoff. She looked over at Bea, who seemed to be enjoying every moment. *Good for her. I am too.*

The nice lady who was the stewardess was very interested in seeing that the ladies were completely comfortable, distributed soft drinks and juice to them during flight, and spoke to them each time she went up and down the aisle.

A trip from Pittsburgh, Pennsylvania, to New York City is not very long. The airplane leveled out for only about twenty minutes, long enough for the stewardess to check on everyone, and before they knew it, the pilot was announcing that they were about to start descending and that no one would be permitted to stand during the next period until landing.

The passengers of the band were a bit disappointed that it was over so fast. This was a good experience for all of them, but they would have another opportunity in the days ahead for the flight back home. It was all so wonderful that it could be accomplished so quickly. They would have been in an automobile or bus for hours and hours. This was the way to go!

Buckle up!

The airplane began the descent, and Julia was now fascinated with looking out the window. Below she could see a shoreline, lots and lots of buildings, bridges, and not many trees. The plane circled the airport once and landed without any problems.

"Please do not unfasten your seatbelt until you are told it is safe to do so" was announced. So they all just waited until the airplane drove on the runway into the place of arrival.

It was wonderful. Julia loved it. Everyone did. If the trip went that smoothly, it was going to be one special trip for the band.

ϒϒϒ

The ladies were the first to get off of the airplane. They all walked together down the outdoor tunnel to the door to Kennedy International. The door opened for them, and there, smiling, were two women with placards large enough for anyone to read: The Band of Hope.

The ladies were young and looked very smart in business attire. In this heat, business attire was lightweight skirts, heeled sandals, stylish hair, and excessive makeup, and they were skinny as rails. The band members assumed that they were to go to where the signs were, and they were right. These were the greeters from FBN, and they would be with them throughout their time in New York City to be sure that they had no problems going to and fro and would be enjoying themselves.

"Welcome to New York City," they said.

The ladies joined up with them, and they all went to a designated area with them.

"We are so happy to see you. I'm Sissy, and this is Patty. We are employees of FBN and have been chosen to assist you at all times during your adventures here in the Big Apple. How was the flight?"

Everyone spoke, saying words such as "Fine," "Wonderful," "Great."

"We're very happy to hear that. We should go to baggage and get your suitcases, and the limousine will be waiting outside that area. I have two drivers here from the airport transport, ready to drive you in their vehicles to Baggage. Come along. Here, let me take your music case," Patty said to Pauline.

All the members of the band froze up. NO ONE touched Pauline's trombone. What was she going to do now?

Pauline looked very much like she knew exactly what to say as she said, "Of course, thank you."

The ladies all looked at one another, lifting their brows and turning their heads. This was a first for Pauline, but she did know right from wrong and certainly did the right thing here.

Soon all the luggage and the ladies were riding on the vehicles through the airport. They felt like royalty. They were thinking it is a good thing that they were given the opportunity to ride, because the baggage collection area seemed like a long drive but quite interesting. The airport was very modern and classy. They couldn't take it all in but knew they would be back.

Before entering the baggage area, they were once again caused to undergo security; however, no one was stopped for any reason this time.

Patty and Sissy led them to the proper pickup, and every time a piece belonging to one of the ladies came out, one of those lovely helpers picked up the luggage and stood it beside its owner. That didn't take long, and now there were two more airport vehicles ready to drive them out through the doors to an awaiting limousine! Ah, the joy of it all.

The limo driver practically bowed to them and invited them all in. He would gather up the luggage. Pauline carefully went in last as she wanted to be certain that the trombone was handled correctly and put in place in the back. She used the excuse of digging through her purse for something she seemed to be missing.

She was still standing behind the limo and saw the trombone being put in, when she looked up and saw Patty beside her.

"Did you lose something?" she asked.

"I thought I did, but everything is fine. I found it."

"Well, that's good. Are you ready then to get in?

"Oh yes. I hope I didn't cause a delay here. I certainly didn't mean to."

"No, no. We are absolutely in grand order. Here, you can sit near the front with me."

At that, Pauline sat down and felt that she was ready and should give the order to go but thought better of it. Her acting sometimes took over reality, and she needed to be aware of that when it happened; therefore, she left the lady-of-the-city posture and sat down to enjoy the ride the same as her dear friends.

"Ladies, we have cold soft drinks and snacks of many sorts for your pleasure. Please do not hesitate to take advantage of all that is here for you," said Sissy.

They were calmed down a bit and the limo was elegant yet comfy, with seats that adjusted to one's desires, and each had somewhat of a decent view of the outside from the windows. They found snacks and drinks to their liking, and Anne asked where they would be going. Sissy answered that they would go down the Queens Midtown Expressway to the Queens Tunnel under the East River. That would get them to Midtown Manhattan to their hotel. The driver turned out of the airport and circled around the airport to get to the Queens Midtown Expressway. The ladies were overwhelmed with the traffic and were happy that the driver was an expert in such situations and conditions.

The drive took them through a residential district before coming to the area of the East River. They were in traffic several lanes across as the driver approached the tunnel. He stopped and paid the fee and worked his way to be the next one entering the tunnel. They had no idea how wide the river was, but it was a short ride to daylight once more. The tunnel had been built in the 1940s to assist the traffic on the bridges. Apparently, it was used constantly, but the traffic did not go quite as fast through, which the ladies found a bit easier to tolerate.

They exited onto East Thirty-Seventh Street in Manhattan. Sissy said they would be travelling to Lexington Avenue on Thirty-Seventh Street. The buildings were sky-high, which they expected, but nonetheless were overpowering as the ladies tried to see the tops from the limousine but couldn't. They turned onto Lexington Avenue, and Sissy said they were on the Seventy-Ninth Street Transverse to Columbus Avenue, where they would find their hotel. The television station was also on Columbus Avenue, which would be convenient when they go to rehearse and to perform.

"FBN likes to work with the accommodations of the Queen Isabel Hotel nearby. It is a lovely hotel with a spacious and ornate Spanish interior, which may be somewhat uncharacteristic of your style, but you will find the food delicious and the rooms up-to-date and very comfortable. Our guests have told us that the hotel was perfect for their visit and for their needs. We often take our customers there for lunch, away from the usual fast foods and hurry-up normalcy of city customs.

"If you look to your right, you will see the building that houses our television station. See, the red brick one there? Yes, the one with the red awning over the entry."

They couldn't see it really, but they got an idea of where it was, because in no time they were turning to the hotel parking. So Sissy was right. It was very close.

39

High Living

They were driven to the front entrance of the hotel and were met immediately by the attendant.

They did not have to worry about a thing. Patty had advised them to just get out of the limo and go inside. Their luggage would be brought in. They were already assigned their rooms, so they would identify their own luggage and they would be taken to rooms on the eighth floor.

They entered the spacious grand entry, which had no resemblance to any hotel in the Pittsburgh area. The two doors opened up to a room with terracotta-tiled flooring with a very high ceiling. The walls were of stucco, with many paintings, especially a very large one of Christopher Columbus that was hung behind what appeared to be the registration desk. All furniture was ornately carved, and the chairs and settees were covered in various floral designs. The chandeliers were black iron, in character with the ironwork seen on the windows and doors as well.

They noticed that every door and window in the two-level grand entry was designed with curved tops, and there were set-in shelves around the walls in the same design. Those shelves held interesting sculptures and vases of flowers.

Patty and Sissy spoke to the attendant, and each lady identified her own luggage. They all went into the sleek-looking elevator and were quickly on the eighth floor. Patty led them to a receiving area of sorts and paired them off as they had previously requested for roommates.

Down the well-lighted and lovely hallway they went to the first room, which was designated for Janine and Julia, and across from them would be Iola and Anne. The next rooms down the hallway were for Pauline and Bea on the left and Marcia and Rachael on the right. The luggage was all distributed easily as they brought what they thought they needed.

The attendant placed the bags conveniently on the suitcase benches and indicated where they could hang their belongings and how to use the freely provided and well-stocked refrigerator. They were each also provided with the entry key and shown how to use them. That was good, because it sure was not what they were used to.

When the beautiful and heavy draperies were opened, they knew for sure they were in New York City! My goodness! There were miles and miles of sky-high buildings. The streets were bustling with taxis zooming lane to lane, and people were quickly moving along the sidewalks everywhere. It was amazing and exciting.

They knew they were not on their own with Patty and Sissy rooming in the fifth room on the floor as well, and that was extremely comforting. How on earth could they ever manage by themselves in this bewildering muddle of motion? Everything was under control. Mr. Harris knew what he was doing, and they would just follow instructions. Thank goodness.

Patty had suggested to them that they unpack, wash up, and meet for lunch downstairs in the lobby. They were all in favor of that.

As they were leaving their rooms, they switched rooms with those across the hall just for a few minutes to see the view from the other side. Everyone had a view such as they had never seen before. They were all enthusiastic and pointing out various sights and going on and on; but it was time to eat and they knew it, so they ambled back toward the elevators.

Anne, who was the world traveler, assumed the role of leader for the time being. She saw to it that they were all on the elevator, pushed the button to the lobby, and everyone else kept talking.

The dining room was beyond expectations. They knew that they were going to be amazed with everything and every sight and every place they went, but they were unable to be nonchalant and laid-back at this point. Yes, they were country folks in the city, and they weren't going to pretend to be anything else—except Pauline, of course!

She suddenly became Lady Paulette, the Socialite. She was walking around, wearing a silk Spanish scarf over her shoulders, with her head in the air—or in the clouds— pretending to be just where she was supposed to be.

Bea was watching her very closely—a bit critically, actually. This was her cousin, and she knew how she was. She was in one of her roles at the moment.

So what? Bea decided. *Let her enjoy herself. She is usually alone, just like we are most of the time. She can be whatever she wants to be, so long as she stays with us and doesn't go wandering off.*

Everyone caught on to Lady Paulette, and they just let her be happy. Why not?

The ladies were hungry and enjoyed especially delicious food. They only ordered what was understandable, and if it wasn't, they asked questions concerning the menu. They didn't want to get indigestion or heartburn, although Bea had enough Tums to share if necessary. So did Marcia, who came equipped for any situation with these wonderful women.

They were ready for a little rest.

The bus tour was scheduled for about two hours later, which was certainly considerate by whoever planned that— maybe Mr. Harris.

By the time they returned to their rooms, no one wanted to talk anymore but rather knew the necessity of rest before the tour began.

40

See for Yourself

Sissy called the rooms, checking to see if everyone was prepared to leave. She reminded each of them to take her room key and lock the door, and they did and met the gals in the hallway.

Paulette the Socialite, using good sense, left her scarf behind and decided to be Pauline for this period of time. Now she could *ooh* and *aah* with the rest of them.

With a nice rest and refreshments, they were ready to be picked up by the hop-on, hop-off tour bus.

There were some people already in the seats, and they tried their best to grab windows yet stay close together. After a very short time, they realized that the upper deck would be better. Sissy told them there were seats available and the view was terrific, so the driver sat still while they moseyed up the stairs and sat down. Wow! The upper deck was all glass and air conditioned as was the lower deck, of course. This was great as long as no one suffered car sickness. A little swaying here and there occurred, and no one noticed. The driver was used to driving very slowly and making stops every so often, so they were comfortable with the arrangements, but no one could plan or predict the fantastic view right down into the midst of it all. They were on top of the world and happy.

They drove down Fifth Avenue along Central Park. To their left were beautiful buildings that could be apartments or offices. They decided that only the extreme rich would be living there. On the right was Central Park, which was much bigger than any imagined. They were astounded that such a place was located right in the middle of the largest city in America. They didn't want to get off the bus at this point, although a few riders did do that, and during the stop, a few more came on board.

The bus continued down Fifth Avenue, through a beautiful, bustling business district of the finest stores, and came to a stop as close to Rockefeller Plaza as it could. They could get off here if they choose and catch the next bus in twenty minutes. They decided to just look around from the great seats they now possessed. Who knew what might be available on the next bus?

The bus turned on Fiftieth Street and passed directly in the vicinity of the picturesque plaza. Some of the ladies would have liked to walk all around the waterfalls and be closer to the famous Atlas statue, and the bronze Prometheus statue. They were thrilled when the fountains on the grounds all exploded into high and low formations together. The dear bus driver slowed down as much as he safely could. He knew he dared not stop completely or he would be severely fined.

They had cameras and did get a few great pictures from their elevated height. They agreed that if they had to pay for this trip, it would be worth it to them. They felt safe and secure in the midst of beauty and madness.

They viewed the Empire State Building from close and afar and knew that they would not go to the top even if they did get off of the bus. So they moved ahead to Times Square and to where they really wanted to go: the site of the World Trade Center.

As they approached the area, they began to relive the horrible scenes they had seen a few years before. Nothing would ever erase those scenes from their minds: the destruction, the fear, the loss of life, and the changes in everyone who saw the reality on the television screens. The site was leveled, and there would soon be renewed interest in memorials in the empty spaces. They would be permitted to walk over to the site today if they wished, but they didn't do it. Perhaps another day, another time, when everything was new again, but not for now. They could only grieve once again and pray to God that nothing like that would happen in America again.

Saint Paul's Chapel stood across the street from the destroyed towers, unscathed. There was deep history in that chapel, which was considered the oldest and longest standing structure in New York City. The driver described the little chapel as a sanctuary for the many workers who for years had worked on clearing the site of the destruction. The ladies were deeply moved and impressed.

They had passed Times Square, where everyone gathered on New Year's Eve and for many other large events. They had the advantage of looking over their shoulders and all around to see the wild and crazy part of the city with neon lights and a myriad of colors all along the street.

They had already spent near to an hour in the bus and now were on their way to Battery Park. If all went well, they would be in a position to see the Statue of Liberty from there. If not, they had decided to just get off the bus and walk to the waterfront, where they would be in a good position to see the Lady.

As they approached the right position, they could barely see her, but they did, at least. The view was quite a distance whether on the bus or not, and so they decided to take the bus back without going any nearer to the water. The decision was made by Julia who was the first to say she hoped she would see the Statue of Liberty. Her parents had come through this area from Hungary so long ago, and she could almost feel them looking out over the waters with her. It was enough to be there for once in her life, and she was grateful for the opportunity.

"It's fine and wonderful right from here. I see it, and I see the boats and the waters over which she is lifting her head in welcome. Thanks, everyone. I'm totally satisfied," Julia said.

It was best that they not stay any longer. The trip back to the hotel would probably be another hour of wonderful sights to see through Greenwich Village, Little Italy, past the United Nations building, etc. They were very pleased with the tour.

Coming back to the hotel, they were talking and talking about New York. They felt different somehow. They gained something that would be with them forever. They felt that they had a different feeling too about metropolitan life, the diversity of races and faces, and the excitement in the people. They would remember.

Sissy and Patty thanked the driver for a wonderful tour. The ladies thanked him also as they left that part of their experience and turned to the next. They were not tired, just exuberant.

They would rest according to the need of each until dinnertime, afterward they would change into their outfits and be gathered to go to the FBN studio and meet up with those in charge of their immediate future.

41

First Rehearsal

Now the ladies were really nervous. They had handled going through two airports, flying into New York, riding in a limo, settling into a very classy hotel, and being bused all over New York City. What can bother them now?

Rehearsing, that's what!

Janine was thinking, *Now they will be scrutinizing us with a magnifying glass and erasers. Will we live up to their expectations? Will the ladies be their natural selves, or will they be totally intimidated and fall apart and not show the happy side of who they are?*

Will I? she also wondered.

She looked around and saw that they were batting their eyes, scratching their faces and arms, looking very unnerved. "Hey, everyone, you look a bit shook up here," she said.

They were sitting in the lobby of a very big building that housed many businesses. They saw on the directory that FBN had the entire sixteenth floor. No one approached them. Sissy and Patty left for the elevator and told them they would be right back, but they hadn't returned after ten minutes at least, which seemed much longer.

Pauline opened her trombone case for the second time, just to be sure.

Bea checked to see if she had everything too. She kept taking deep breaths, happy at least that she could.

Anne stood up and walked around, pretending to look at something every time she stopped, when in reality, she wasn't looking at anything but just trying to shake the jitters. No one had ever known Anne to be rattled over anything, so they didn't realize that she actually was.

Julia's heart was racing. *Here I am! Yes, here I am in New York City, about to perform before professional people. They have no idea what it feels like to be living in a little tiny town like West Hope and think you have done the greatest thing on earth to have a family and a few good friends. They probably will think we are hicks from the sticks.*

Iola wondered how on earth this could be happening. *I can hardly breathe. I know I'm all right, but I can't sit here another minute without saying something rude. No, no, I won't do that. Oh, please, let's just get on with this.*

They were all nervous, and waiting now was not good.

Several people noticed them gathered together in red blouses, white slacks, and baggage. They all wondered what they were here for. The ladies noticed that people were frowning when they passed by.

Sissy appeared finally.

"I'm sorry, I'm truly sorry. I know you must be wondering where I was. It was a trip-up. Everything's okay now. Let's go."

A trip-up? What's that supposed to mean?

No one said anything but gathered their baggage and followed. Janine lifted a couple of them and Marcia did also, and they were on the elevator on their way to the FBN studio.

At the sixteenth floor, the elevator stopped, and Sissy led the delegation down the hall.

There was a door with a glass panel that said FBN.

Oh boy!

They entered, and Mr. Harris met them right away. That was good. They felt just a tiny bit better.

"Ladies, ladies, you look wonderful, and it's good to see you again. Come in."

"I want you to meet The Band of Hope," he said to those in the office.

Turning to the ladies, he said, "This is Mr. Irvin, who will be your state manager, and this is Ms. Marks who is our great director. They will be working with you this evening to arrange for the production tomorrow."

Ms. Marks floated across the floor and extended her hand to each and every one of them. She looked classy and well-dressed, and she spoke with clarity and charm. They knew they were with a well-educated and talented person.

Is that good or bad? We're certainly not talented, and she's gonna find that out real quick, thought Bea.

"Ladies, this is such a wonderful treat. I have heard such fine things about your mission and your experiences, and I enjoyed the tape we have of the interviews conducted in West Hope. We will be using some of those to open our show tomorrow as a perfect introduction to who you are and what you do in service to others and for the Lord.

"Don't be nervous. All we want from you tonight is to go through the normal routine as you always do. You will have an audience tonight of some of folks from a senior home right here in New York. They have the same dreams that you have. They have the same losses you've had too. Some are disabled, and some are unhappy. I want you to entertain them with all that you have, because they need a great uplifting tonight. They need to feel hope, and I know from what I've seen that you are very good at spreading hope to others.

"You know our mission here at FBN is to bring as many people to Christ as possible. You have the same mission in the perfect way that you've been called to do. Don't change a thing. What you do works for you, and we want others to know that."

She was so lovely and said just the right things to the ladies. They were relaxing on the spot.

Mr. Irvin was to show them how to come out from behind the curtain. He took the CD that Janine had made for him. Someone would be watching her the entire time for cutoffs and starts. However, Janine suggested that the sound manager just stop the disk after every song, and when she announced to the audience the next number that the music would automatically be started then. If that doesn't work well, it can be corrected for the next time.

Mr. Irvin liked this lady. She had it figured out well. That was good reasoning, and that's what they would do.

Janine usually announced the coming of the ladies from behind the curtain. She discussed this with the director and the stage manager, and they thought that she should lead the band out after the announcer introduced the band's appearance.

"Sure, let's try that," Janine said.

She was beginning to feel confident and comfortable. She went over to the ladies and asked them to put their instruments in place out on the stage. Janine had no idea where the audience was. She and the band were still behind a very heavy stage curtain. This was really interesting and felt like *ShowTime*.

So the ladies went to the chairs placed for them and set up their props and instruments. It was decided that they would all go to the stage left, march out in a line in front of the curtain to "When the Saints Go Marching In," and when they were all there, the curtains would move open for the audience to finally see them.

Janine loved the idea. The ladies did too. They were feeling calmer and were looking forward to their time on the big stage.

ϓϓϓ

Of all things! There was a makeup lady. She came over to them offstage and suggested that they go into the makeup room. They should see them under the lights with makeup tonight so that they would know exactly what to do tomorrow.

"Stage lights really fade out the complexions. Everyone needs much more color than they would ever suppose. Don't be alarmed if you look at one another and see deeper and brighter colors on your faces. The lights will fade those colors quite quickly."

They took their turns and had makeup applied to redden cheeks and lips. They looked at one another and got the giggles. They didn't look too bad. Ha!

Now they were in their costumes—with aprons, crazy-looking hats, and horns with kazoos—and ready to go. Janine joined them. She liked that. Never before had she had the opportunity to be right there but was always talking about them first to the audience.

The stage manager, Mr. Irvin, came over and said that they should be very quiet because the technologist said he could hear them through the very sensitive and massive microphone system they are using. And he said not to worry about using any kind of microphone when they talked to one another in the routine. "Everything you say and do will be picked up by our system."

Well, that was good, but it also was a bit of caution by him.

They stood very quietly from that moment on.

The producer of the show, Mr. Keys, came on the stage, and he gave the finest introduction ever heard. The ladies could now hear that there was, in fact, an audience because when he finished, he asked for them to clap in welcome to The Band of Hope.

The music started!

Janine smiled at them and turned and led with head held high and her director's wand (a plastic spoon) in hand as she marched along. When she found that they were all in the line where they were supposed to be, she stopped. They stopped, and the massive curtain lifted.

She did not know that the screen behind had been dropped down to a bright, beautiful country scene, very much like the scene they see every day at home. How beautiful! How appropriate too! She wished the ladies could see how great they looked under the stage lights with the colorful background and their big, beautiful smiles.

She almost cried. Instead she took in as deep of a breath as she could, and said in her heart, *Thank you, Lord. Help us to be all that we can be for Your glory and honor.*

When the music stopped, they heard a roar of applause from the audience. Well, how about that?

They knew why they were there. It all took on a new meaning from rehearsal to being the deliverers of hope and joy to others. They were fine. No, they were wonderful. The audience enjoyed them, the managers in the wings were enjoying them, and everything was as it was supposed to be.

At the close of the performance, they sang together with the audience, "God Bless America," and they could hear the enthusiasm from the audience, from the stage—from sea to shining sea. It was fantastic. Janine and all the ladies were overwhelmed with the sharing and knew that they would do well tomorrow night. It was what they needed. They would enjoy everything from now on without worry.

At the end of the show, the house lights were on, and they had the opportunity to see the audience. They were so cheerful and wanted to great them face-to-face. Ms. Marks gave her permission for a few of them to come on stage and shake hands with the ladies, and they were so happy to do that. Some asked them for autographs! *My heavens!*

When the audience left, some in wheelchairs, some being assisted by caretakers, they were happy as could be. The Band of Hope accomplished a mission again. Praise God.

Ms. Marks talked with Janine and the band. She said that they were not going to cut anything out of what the band usually did. They had planned on cutting down to twenty-three minutes, but if they did that, they would have to cut the final patriotic number, and it was far too important to do that. They could and would cut a bit of the introduction, and Mr. Keys will move through his introduction at a better pace. The show would be one hour.

That night the production personnel would go through the interviews, time the show, and lay it out for the entire hour.

Ms. Marks said, "We are very excited to present your program in its entirety. You have a wonderful program. I am very happy to have it sent around the country. Thank you all for all you do in your community and region. Thank you for agreeing to come here and letting us show many others what can be done for the Lord with the gifts He has given to you."

Mr. Harris was there too and was smiling ear to ear.

"Ladies, ladies, we are so happy for you and for our station as well. I hope you are having a good time here in New York City. Tomorrow you will be going to a Broadway show, the matinee of *Mamma Mia!* You should really enjoy it, and it will be something lighthearted that will make you laugh and have fun. Then get some rest, have a nice dinner, and enjoy the performance tomorrow night. I know that's going to all be wonderful for you."

They were excited to go see *Mamma Mia!* They were completely happy and hence relieved. They had no worries now.

Bea was sure she was feeling fine and well, and she only had one day to go. *What more can I want? I'm happier than I ever thought I'd be at this age—or any age.*

Pauline was thrilled to be on stage. It was her dream. When those lights came on, she knew she was where she was supposed to be all along.

Rachael was well again and didn't need any walking assistance. Her smile was real; she was overflowing with hope for the coming days and years. After all, she has a job to do with the band.

Anne thought being with The Band of Hope was the best thing she had ever done, and it was far, far away from any lifestyle she ever thought she'd want. She even liked the makeup tonight.

Iola tried to believe that she was still doing the Lord's will. She was very straitlaced, and this was harder for her to do than it was for anyone else. When she picked up the little brown jug tonight, she said a short prayer that the Lord would see her as the good person she always wanted and tried hard to be. She left it at that and proceeded through the routine knowing what was in her heart.

Julia was bursting with happiness. Her brain was whirling into one thought and then another. *God is good,* she thought.

Marcia wondered how in the world she ever got in with this beautiful group. She didn't really associate with the ladies. She wasn't as old as they are. She just felt the nudge. Janine said to her that sometimes the Holy Spirit just nudges us to do something that is meant for the betterment of the kingdom.

I believe it. How many times has the Lord spoken to me and I didn't listen? I'm going to work very hard at being close to the Lord and listen to Him. He knows what's best. He knows what's needed, obviously. From now on, I won't mistake His calling.

Janine knew.

She had known for quite some time. God's plan for her life became very clear a few years back. She has followed His call, and she was happy. What could be better?

Thank you, Lord. You have given me so much. I pledge my all to you, forever!

42

Curtains Up!

Did anyone sleep last night? Apparently everyone did, because the ladies were up and hustling about like younger folks, humming tunes and happy. Patty and Sissy met them for breakfast at the appointed time in the dining room. They were now familiar with the hotel and the elevator. A beautiful breakfast buffet was placed out for the dining guests, and it was just the thing for the hungry ladies. They could pick and choose without worry.

Seated around a nicely appointed table, they reviewed the events of the day before with cheerful recall. There was not a thing to complain about, and they felt so at ease with the people from FBN.

They would not be going to the theater until around 12:30 p.m., so they decided to have a very light breakfast, eat a lighter lunch at 11:00 a.m., and be ready for *Mamma Mia!*

Pauline was with them, but she was not actually with them. Pauline is now Petrula, a famous Broadway dancer. So she entered the dining hall in a floating fashion, with an air of importance about herself. She joined the ladies, but she felt uncomfortable because they were not part of her usual theater acquaintances. She fussed with her napkin, looked at her fingernails (which had been manicured two days ago), and kept looking over her shoulder to others in the room.

She appeared to be expecting someone to come up to her and discuss the theater and worldly events with her.

Finally, she asked Bea if she thought some of her friends would be at the theater today, and Bea, looking at the others around the table, said she didn't know.

"Well, of course they will be. They attend the theater constantly," Petrula said.

Bea leaned over to Marcia and said, "Here we go. She has decided to be Petrula instead of Pauline at this point."

Marcia leaned over to Janine. "Is this going to be a problem?"

"I don't think so. She's pretending. She knows what she's doing. She just loves to act a part. We'll all watch her carefully. She has never gone over the boundaries of sanity. Her family sees this all the time, and so do we. We can enjoy it with her or get ourselves all upset. It's more fun to play along."

"Okay, I didn't know," said Marcia.

Sissy and Patty asked them if they would like to take a stroll around the building.

"Is it safe?" Iola asked.

"I wouldn't worry. The security guard here agreed to walk with us anyway. He's pretty intimidating to look at. We'll be fine. This is a safer part of the city than some others that you hear about. I've walked from place to place many times and usually walk to work at the studio by myself without any interference," Patty said.

Sissy injected, "If you don't want to do that, its fine."

The ladies were all for it. They had seen Mr. Security Guard and knew that they would not be approached in any way with him along.

"Good, I'll tell you what. Don't go dangling a purse on your shoulder. That just makes sense. Cross the strap over the opposite shoulder if you have a bag like that, or lock it in the safely locked box provided by the hotel. See? Over there behind the registrar."

They prepared themselves. Patty alerted Mr. Security Guard, and off they went.

His name was really Barry MacGrogan, and the ladies called him Mr. MacGrogan. He was certainly Irish—friendly, ruddy-complexioned, and kindly by nature.

They felt safe. He suggested they go around the side of the building and see that they were located right on the corner of the streets. How interesting. The buildings were all skyscrapers around, but some were shorter than others. Most of them had small businesses occupying the street-level floors. They saw clothing, shoes, jewelry—all very fashionable and with out-of-reach prices, most likely.

They turned around and walked in the direction of the station. This was the main street for traffic, and everywhere were taxis. Little orange machines darting in and out, toot-tooting along. It almost seemed like a little boy's dream world. There was noise, action, and electricity in the air.

Petrula felt right at home. She walked elegantly along, and they all kept an eye on her. She wanted to go into the shoe store. There was discussion among them, and they all decided to go along with her rather than leave her on her own. So in they went.

Petrula found shoes she wanted to try on. Oh dear! The employee measured her foot and came back with that shoe and several others of the same heel size and appearance. She tried both shoes in each pair and walked around as though they were perfect for her. She kept it up with different shoes for a while, as the ladies stood then sat while waiting.

Here was a red pair that she was determined to purchase. She had brought along her purse and asked the price of the shoe. That was the moment of lucidity for Petrula, who decided that she had several pair of red shoes at home.

She walked out and said, "I enjoyed that. I knew I wouldn't purchase anything today, but I'm glad I had the occasion to try on shoes in that particular place. I'll just keep them in mind, and maybe another day here in the city would be better. We have too much to do today."

The moment was shared then and evermore.

They had a very fine, leisurely walk, and just down the street they saw the FBN sign. They turned back to the hotel because they could not walk that distance without feeling tired. They would be back there tonight, and they were looking forward to it with the most joyful expectation ever.

When they arrived back to the hotel, Mr. MacGrogan took each lady's hand and almost bowed to them as he said he enjoyed the time together. He reminded them not to leave the building alone. He hoped they would be enjoying the rest of their stay in the city.

"Now, wasn't he nice?" said Bea.

"Good Irish fella," said Rachael.

Pauline was with them now. They talked about maybe resting just a bit before eleven o'clock, and it was agreed.

ΥΥΥ

Now they were back in the limousine. They felt comfortable and natural this time as they were driving down Broadway to the theater.

Pauline knew where they were going, and it was the biggest moment so far of the entire trip for her. She would feel right at home with stage lights, busy theatergoers, ushers—all of which were components of the life she knew she was born to be a part of and that one day she would. Well, here she was!

Sissy and Patty had the tickets and so they were led inside. How beautiful! The theater lobby was so lush in velvets, tassels, carpets, and brass. A huge chandelier was spread out over their heads, and they walked through feeling excited and knowing they were going to have a very special time.

Their personal attendants led them to their seats, which were excellent, and they were all in a row together. Patty and Sissy would be behind them so that they could be sure the ladies were doing fine and assist if they needed anything at all.

Not one of them had ever been treated so finely. How could this be?

Patty had asked if they needed anything. No one could think of a thing. They had programs and were looking over the names. Since they weren't ever in a Broadway theater, everything was new to them.

Petrula sat still and watched the curtains. She seemed to be in a different world with her thoughts, but she was not giving anyone cause for concern.

The lights began to dim, the audience quieted down, the orchestra began to play, and soon the curtain was lifted to an unbelievable scene of business. They were entranced throughout the entire play.

The music was fantastic, the acting was superb, and it was so funny! They laughed and laughed and had a great afternoon. What fun! No wonder people loved going to see these plays. They were gigantic productions! Thousands of dollars went into each and every detail. It all pays off.

They were so interested that no one noticed Petrula leaving.

During intermission, Patty asked if Petrula had gone to the restroom, and all the ladies began to wonder when and where Petrula had gone.

Oh no! The houselights were on, so Patty and Sissy said they were going to go looking for her and suggested that the rest stay where they were for now.

The ladies were very concerned. How could they not see her leave? They were certainly deeply involved in the production. She must have eased herself out of the row to the other side. She had been the first one to her seat, so she was to the left of all of them. Why did they let her sit there?

Patty and Sissy split up with cell phones, one in one direction and one in the other. First place first—the restrooms. No Petrula.

How about the balcony? She was not there!

Surely, surely she did not go outside. They just couldn't imagine that, but they asked the doorkeeper and he had not seen anyone leave, so that was good.

Now what?

They suddenly thought of going backstage. No one was permitted backstage, but why not Petrula? She could very well have done it.

They were stopped immediately. They explained as best they could about the lady they were looking for, and the doorman there said she did come by him. He thought she was one of the cast, the way she carried herself. He didn't ask for identification. He should have, of course, but she gave every indication that she needed to be back there right away.

Sissy looked at Patty, and they both had permission to go find her.

After looking around at the conglomerate of costume changes, props, etc., they found her in a group of people discussing something or other about changing costumes quickly for one of the upcoming scenes.

She was advising them. They were listening.

My goodness!

Patty inched her way over to Petrula and said, "Oh, my dear Petrula, how wonderful to see you. When did you arrive?"

Petrula was pretending again and fell right into Patty's conversation as though she had planned it that way.

"It's good to see you too." She turned to the group and told them she really had to get on with some important business, and they just let her go.

"Break a leg," she said.

"Thanks!"

"This way, dear," Sissy said.

The three of them walked down the sidehalls to the lobby and then down the aisle to join the other ladies just as intermission was over.

"Hello, everyone, are we ready for the second act?" asked Petrula.

The ladies played along, but she would not get away again. Later Sissy and Patty told them the story, and they just shook their heads. That was Petrula, all right.

43

Go Forth!

The rest of the afternoon went just fine. The ladies were troubled with what to do about Petrula, a.k.a. Pauline, but Petrula just disappeared and Pauline was fine about it.

Finally they were taken back to FBN for their performance. So many of the staff there wanted to meet the ladies, and they visited for a time with several of them.

Janine was alert to just exactly what had to be done. She wanted to be sure that the chairs were in the right places with enough space between for the instruments. She and the stage manager walked through all that. Everything was ready.

The ladies were smiling in a row and were ready also. This was their big opportunity to do even more than they dreamed possible to promote Christian living as a great joy. They were eager to do it, and the time had come.

Janine was first in line. She turned and looked into the eyes of Pauline, a.k.a. Petrula, a.k.a. whoever. She saw how happy she was. She had that trombone and was ready. Janine whispered in her ear, "Break a leg." Petrula nodded and smiled.

Janine stepped up to Anne next and touched her shoulder. Elegant, lovely, Anne. *God bless her. She is one of the finest ladies I have ever known. My life is blessed to have known her.*

Next, she joined with Iola. Taking her hands, Janine said, "Thank you." Iola didn't ask why, she just smiled in return.

Bea was looking good, so alive, so eager. Holding her hands, Janine shed a tear. She couldn't help it. Her love for all of them was so deep, so real, that she was having difficulty holding back. Bea loved her back with a good ol' hug.

Marcia looked at Janine as they met there face-to-face, both knowing that they were truly in God's hands tonight.

Then Rachael, who had given up any hope for meaningful living, now stood before her with that beautiful smile, exuding her appreciation of living in this moment with a clear understanding now of why she was still here.

Julia, her Julia, was the one God had chosen as Janine's mentor. Janine was so thankful for her and so loving toward her, she could only embrace her and say "Thank you." Julia didn't understand how Janine felt that way, when all along it was Janine who *led her* out of the darkness.

Janine walked back to the front, overflowing with love and hope, as Mr. Keys walked to center stage for the introduction of her lovely ladies.

The house lights dimmed, and one light shone upon him for the time being. He said, "FBN is always pleased to bring good news of ordinary people doing great things for the Lord, because we all know that we are *all* ordinary until God changes us for His purpose, and then miracles happen—they really do.

"You have seen the interviews that we have had with these remarkable ladies. You've seen them in real life in their neighborhoods. They are not larger-than-life, but even in their senior years they are living lives enlarged by God.

"Tonight we will see the results of them coming together at the Lord's bidding and becoming one of the most entertaining and successful groups we have come across. The Band of Hope from the little town of West Hope, Pennsylvania, has been spreading the love, joy, and hope of the Lord throughout a small region of Western Pennsylvania for a number of years and has touched hundreds of lives. We know that their enthusiasm will touch you tonight. Watch and see what the Lord will do when we have the faith to go forth in His Name on the pathway He has chosen for us.

"Please join me in welcoming The Band of Hope to our stage tonight."

They heard their music over the clapping, the lights came on, the curtain lifted, and the ladies joyfully entered, marching to the rhythm of God's glorious master plan.

The End

Since the writing of this story has taken years to completion, I have had your comments along the way as you have had to wait for this last book. How wonderful you are, dear readers. You have told me that you feel love for these characters as I do and are eager to learn more about them. This has encouraged me; so page after page as I have written for the joy of being alive with my beloved characters, I have written to give you pure pleasure as you bring them back into your homes and into your lives again as well.

May God bless you all! . . . . Mary Jean